BLACK EROTICA 2

MORE EROTIC, ADULT SHORT STORIES WRITTEN BY BLACK WOMEN FEATURING OLDER-YOUNGER, BDSM, FIRST TIMES, ANAL SEX, GROUPS, CUCKOLD, GANGBANGS, MFM, LESBIAN, AND PARANORMAL

JADE ST. JAMES

CONTENTS

INTRODUCTION

Well, you asked for it! I got such a great response from my previous collection, Black Erotica, that I knew I had to bring my queens another volume.

Like last time, I contacted my favorite black and BIPOC writers and told them to write the kind of stories they would love to read. And they did not disappoint!

This new volume has more of the things you liked from the first: sensual stories about us, written by us.

Enjoy yourself, my friends. Alone with a glass of wine or with your partner!

With all my love and admiration,

Jade

1

BACK TO SCHOOL

BY SANDRA WELLS

If there was one thing Ebony dreaded more than failing, it was the holidays. For others, it was always partying or camping. But for her, it was a time to work her ass off. After all, her mom wasn't earning much despite working three shifts. And her dad? He was still ruing his days at the Navy before he got discharged for disobeying his commanding officer. So summer breaks were meant for only one thing: work.

Ebony met with her friend Amber at their favorite diner in town. Amber was her go-to for anything she needed. She'd helped her when she first lost her tooth. She'd been there when she broke her leg for the first time riding a bicycle. The first time Ebony saw a stain she didn't fully understand, Amber was there to explain what it was. It was hard to picture an eighteen-year-old girl like Amber with so much knowledge within her reach. But if your parents were writers who forced you to read a lot, you would have a lot of knowledge too.

"Hey Amber, how are you?" Ebony said, greeting her friend with a hug.

"I'm good, thanks. How about you?" Amber replied, returning the hug.

"I'm good too, but I'm looking for a summer job. Do you know of any openings?"

"Well, my sister's friend is looking for a babysitter for her two kids over the summer. She pays well, and you'll have plenty of free time during the day while the kids are at camp," Amber suggested.

Ebony smiled. Trust Amber to always know someone with a job opening.

"I don't have much experience with kids, but I'll take anything just to earn some money," she said, nodding.

"Don't worry; the kids are pretty easy to care for. Plus, it's a great opportunity to gain some experience and earn some cash," Amber said with a smile.

"Okay, can you give me her contact information? I'll reach out to her and see if we can set up an interview," Ebony said, feeling relieved that she had a lead.

"Sure, I'll send you her number and email address. Good luck, and let me know how it goes!" Amber said, giving Ebony a pat on the back.

It was a bright and sunny day in the city as Ebony walked up the steps to the large house she had been directed to. It was a beautiful bungalow with flowers blooming in a small garden. She was excited to start her new job and couldn't wait to meet the children she would look after.

Ebony heard the sound of children laughing and playing inside as she rang the doorbell. The door opened, and a woman greeted her warmly.

"Ebony, right?" the woman asked with a giant smile.

"Yes, ma'am. Good afternoon."

"Please, come in," the woman said, turning.

Ebony could feel the warmth in the house the moment she walked in. There were hanging pictures of the family all over the wall. An antique table was in the sitting room where the woman had asked her to wait. Ebony looked around, admiring the artwork on a shelf and the picture of a rhinoceros spaciously occupying a portion of the wall to her right.

The woman showed up again with two kids trailing behind her. One of them looked very timid and soft. Ebony could tell the second one was the terror of the house. Her hair was messy, and her shoelaces were dragging behind her.

"Kids, this is Ebony. She's going to be our babysitter for the summer," the woman said, introducing Ebony to her children.

"Hi, I'm Ebony," she said, smiling at the children. "I'm your new babysitter. It's great to meet you both." She knelt to their level.

Sharon was an energetic 10-year-old with long brown hair and bright green eyes. Caleb was a gentle eight-year-old with curly black hair and a sweet smile.

"Hi, Ebony!" the children chimed in unison, grinning from ear to ear.

As the woman showed Ebony around the house and showed her the children's toys and books, Ebony could feel her excitement growing. She was eager to start playing with the children and helping them with their homework. But beyond that, she stared at the magnificent man working on a PC in the corner of the house.

She had heard him speak on the phone, but up close, she felt drawn to his masculinity. He was well-toned, taller than her boyfriend, Bryan, and had a face only the angels in heaven could have sculpted. If he were a meal, she would want to eat him every day of her life.

"Did I even tell you my name?" the woman asked suddenly.

Ebony snapped out of her daydream.

"Yes, ma'am," she replied hurriedly. "You're Mrs. Green."

"Please, call me Johanna. That's my husband, Sean," she added while nodding toward the man. "He spoke with you on the phone."

"Hello, Mr. Green," Ebony said.

"It's Sean," he replied without taking his eyes off the monitor.

Ebony felt something wet between her legs the moment he spoke. She blushed slightly, hiding her face so the man's wife wouldn't notice.

"Okay, I think I have everything covered," Johanna said. "We'll be back by 9 p.m. If you need anything, don't hesitate to call us."

"Thank you," Ebony replied, feeling grateful for the opportunity. "I'm looking forward to spending time with the children."

As the couple left the house, Ebony began to play with the children. They laughed and giggled as they ran around the house, playing hide-and-seek and dressing up in costumes.

"Can we read a book, Ebony?" the little girl asked, tugging at Ebony's hand.

"Of course," Ebony said, leading the children to the couch. "What book do you want to read?"

The next day, Ebony met Amber at their favorite diner to catch up and tell her friend how her first day as a babysitter had gone. The aroma of freshly brewed coffee and sizzling bacon filled the air as they sat at a cozy booth by the window.

"So how was it?" Amber asked eagerly, taking a sip of her latte.

"It was great," Ebony replied, smiling. "Mrs. Green is super nice, and the kids are so sweet."

"That sounds like so much fun. And you're getting paid for it!" Amber said with a laugh.

"Yeah, I can't believe it," Ebony said, grateful for the job opportunity.

After chatting a bit longer, Ebony said goodbye to Amber and headed to the Green family's house for her second workday. She had packed a bag full of activities and crafts for the kids, eager to keep them entertained throughout the day. When she arrived,

Johanna was busy getting ready for work, and she quickly kissed Sharon and Caleb goodbye before rushing out the door.

"Good luck, Ebony! Have fun with the kids today," Johanna said, waving as she headed to her car.

Ebony smiled and turned to the kids, who were both wearing pajamas and looking a bit sleepy.

"Good morning, guys! Did you sleep well?" Ebony asked, kneeling to their level.

"Yeah, we did. But we're still tired," Sharon said with a yawn.

"Well, let's start the day with some breakfast. How about we make pancakes?" Ebony suggested, getting up from the floor.

Caleb's eyes lit up at the mention of pancakes, and he eagerly followed Ebony to the kitchen. Sharon trailed behind, looking a bit more hesitant. Ebony chatted with the kids about their favorite foods and activities as they mixed the batter and cooked the pancakes. She learned tat Sharon loved to draw and play soccer, while Caleb was obsessed with robots and video games.

After breakfast, Ebony suggested that they do some crafts. She pulled out some colored paper, glue, and scissors, and the kids got to work creating paper crowns and tiaras.

As they worked, Ebony couldn't help but notice how different Sharon and Caleb were. Caleb was organized and meticulous, carefully cutting each piece of paper and gluing it down. On the other hand, Sharon was more impulsive, cutting and gluing with abandon and creating a wild and colorful mess. But despite their differences, Ebony could tell that the kids loved each other deeply. They joked and laughed together, and when Caleb accidentally spilled glue on Sharon's crown, she simply laughed and said it made it look better.

As the day went on, Ebony took the kids to the park, where they ran around and played tag. They explored the woods behind the playground, looking for bugs and squirrels. And they even made a new friend, Lily, who was there with her mom.

When they returned to the house, it was late afternoon, and the kids were getting tired. Ebony suggested they watch a movie, and they all settled on the couch with a bowl of popcorn.

As the movie played, Ebony found herself feeling grateful for the job she had. She had always loved kids, and being a babysitter was the perfect way to spend her summer.

But as she watched the movie, she couldn't help but feel a bit lonely. She had been so busy with the kids that she hadn't had much time to see her friends or go out and do things she enjoyed. A part of her wished Sean was around to keep her company. Then she quickly banished the thought. He was married. She wasn't even sure he could love a girl like her. His wife was more beautiful than she was.

As the movie ended and the kids headed to bed, Ebony cleaned the living room and prepared to head home. But as she was about to leave, Sean walked in the door. Her heart stopped beating for a while. He didn't notice, but she was flustered.

"Hey, Ebony! How was your day?" he asked, smiling at her.

"It was great! The kids were so much fun," Ebony replied, feeling shy around him. She quickly stepped aside so he could get into the house.

"That's good to hear. I'm sorry I wasn't here earlier to help," Sean said, looking a bit regretful.

"Oh, it's no problem. I had it under control," Ebony said, trying to sound confident.

"Well, Johanna won't be here until tomorrow. She has a few things to sort out at work that will take the whole night. Are you sure you don't want to stay a bit longer? I can drop you off."

The offer was tempting, and Ebony nearly jumped in excitement. Instead, she nodded and sat while he went into his room to change.

Ebony couldn't help but feel nervous around Sean as they chatted while he drove her back home. She found herself drawn to him despite knowing it was inappropriate to have feelings for her married employer. He stopped a little distance from her house and asked if he could walk her to the front door.

"That won't be necessary, Mr. Green," Ebony replied. "I'm fine."

"It's Sean," he told her with a wink before driving off.

That night, Ebony stripped herself naked and stood before a mirror. She wondered why she hadn't made a move on him. All the time they were in the car, she'd wanted to kiss him badly. She was so horny that the tingling between her legs drove her mad with desire.

"Snap out of it, Ebony," she said to her reflection in the mirror. "He's married."

But no matter how hard she tried, she couldn't get him out of her head. She imagined him touching her nipples, pinching lightly until she felt a rising surge of pleasure. Her hands trailed down to her thighs, driven by an illusion that Sean's string muscular arms were guiding her to ecstasy.

"Oh, Sean," she moaned softly.

Her fingers found her center folds and spread them open a bit. She cried silently as a surge of pleasure hit her. Then she threw her head back and inserted her index finger into her honeypot. Excitement coursed through her body, mixed with pleasure, desires, and wants. She managed to stifle her moans by biting down on her pillow. She wanted him now more than anything. If only he weren't married.

Six Years Later

Ebony was late to class. She had overslept and woken up feeling tired. There was no time to tidy up. She just grabbed something and ran out of her dorm. She ran so hard that she didn't know when she accidentally bumped into someone. She looked up and was surprised to see Sean standing there, looking just as surprised.

"Sean? Oh my God, it's been years!" Ebony exclaimed, hugging him tightly.

At first, he looked confused. Then he looked closely and recognized her.

"Ebony!" he said with delight. "Been a long time."

Ebony looked up at him. "What happened to you guys?" she asked. "I woke up the next day, and your family was gone. You only left me a note with the neighbor."

"Uh...this is going to be very hard to explain," Sean said with a dry chuckle. "Are you going somewhere?"

"Yes," she replied. "I have a class, and I'm very late."

Her phone chimed. It was a notification from the class group. They had postponed the class.

"Scratch that," she told him quickly. "The class has been canceled."

"Coffee, then?" Sean asked.

There was a café nearby, and they headed toward it.

"I'm sorry about how we disappeared," Sean told her. "I got a new job, and we had to move the next day. It was something we couldn't control."

"It's fine," Ebony replied. "I was just worried."

The café was bustling with students trying to grab a quick meal and lecturers grabbing coffee before class. Sean said hello to a few older students, making short jokes with them.

"You go to school here?" Ebony asked him with surprise.

"Yes. I'm pursuing a master's in education," he replied. "I was busy with life and had to put my education on hold. Now that I'm free...well."

They both ordered coffee. Ebony couldn't keep her eyes off him. Six years ago, he had been a stud with blue eyes and jet-black hair. Even now, despite his age, he still looked like God's most precious creation. The gray hair on his head did nothing to change his handsome face. His smile was as enticing as she remembered it. Memories of that last night flooded back in a frenzy, and she felt her panties get wet.

As they sipped their drinks, Ebony could tell something was wrong.

"What about you?" he asked suddenly. "What are you doing here?"

"I'm a med student," Ebony replied after clearing her throat. "Third year."

"Wow," he said. "Didn't know you were into medicine."

There are so many things you don't know about me, Ebony said to herself.

"Well, here I am," she said out loud. Then she asked about his family.

There was an awkward silence before he answered. His face fell suddenly, and there was a sadness in his eyes like she had never seen before.

"We got divorced," he said, his voice barely above a whisper. "And my wife got custody of the kids."

Ebony felt sadness wash over her as she realized how difficult this must be for him. She listened intently as he poured out his heart, sharing the ups and downs of his marriage and the heartbreak of losing his children.

As Sean spoke, Ebony couldn't help but notice how much he had changed since the last time she'd seen him. He had always been a charismatic and charming guy, but now there was a sadness in his eyes that she couldn't ignore. It was clear that he was going through a tough time.

Despite the heaviness of their conversation, they found themselves laughing and joking. They talked about many things and found that they had a lot in common.

But as they talked, Ebony couldn't shake the feeling that there was something Sean wasn't telling her. She didn't want to pry, but she knew he needed someone to confide in.

After a while, Sean took a deep breath and looked at

her. "There's something else I need to tell you," he said hesitantly.

Ebony nodded, encouraging him to continue.

"I've been struggling a lot with depression," Sean admitted. "It's been tough since the divorce, and I'm barely holding on."

Ebony's heart went out to him. She knew firsthand how difficult it could be to deal with mental health issues, and she could only imagine how much harder it was for Sean with everything else he was going through.

"Have you considered getting help?" she asked gently.

Sean shrugged. "I don't know. It just feels like there's no point. Everything's falling apart, and I don't see how therapy or medication could fix it."

Ebony reached across the table and took his hand.

"It's not about fixing things," she said. "It's about giving you the tools to cope and manage. And there's nothing wrong with needing a little extra support."

"Thanks," he said. "I do feel better after having talked to you."

Ebony only smiled. She was glad that they had met again. Six years ago, she had been a naïve young girl unable to express herself. Not this time. After all, he was no longer married.

"It wasn't my fault, you know. My wife accused me of cheating on her," Sean said, looking down at his coffee cup. "I didn't do it, but she wouldn't believe me. She kept accusing me repeatedly until I couldn't take it anymore."

Ebony reached across the table and placed her hand on Sean's.

"I'm so sorry," she said softly. "That must have been hard for you."

"It was," Sean said, his eyes darkening. "I loved her, but I couldn't take the constant accusations. It was like she didn't even know me."

Ebony nodded, understanding how painful it must have been for Sean to have someone he loved so profoundly not trust him. "Sometimes people can be insecure," she said. "It doesn't mean you did anything wrong."

Sean looked up at Ebony, his eyes searching hers.

"Thank you for saying that," he said. "You always know just what to say."

Ebony smiled, feeling a flutter in her stomach. Ebony found herself getting lost in Sean's deep brown eyes and charming smile as they continued talking. She felt a warmth spreading through her body that she couldn't ignore.

"I had a crush on you back then," Ebony blurted out before she could stop herself. "I just never told you because I didn't think you would feel the same way."

Sean's eyes widened in surprise. "Are you serious?" he asked. "I had no idea."

Ebony felt a rush of embarrassment. Had she just made a fool of herself? But then Sean took her hand and looked deep into her eyes. Then he looked down at his watch and let out a sigh.

"I have to go," he said regretfully. "But let's catch up again soon, okay?"

"Definitely," Ebony said, trying to keep the disappointment from her voice.

As they got up from the table, Sean hesitated

momentarily before facing her. "Ebony," he said softly. "There's something I have to tell you."

"What is it?" Ebony asked, her heart pounding in her chest.

"I find you very attractive," Sean said, his voice low and intense. "I always have."

Ebony felt a surge of excitement mixed with disbelief. Was it possible that Sean felt the same way she did?

"Why didn't you say anything when I said I had a crush on you?" she asked fiercely.

He fumbled for words and decided to shut his mouth when he couldn't find any. She made to go, but he held her hand. "I'm so sorry," he said. "Can we go somewhere private to talk about this better?"

Ebony sighed deeply. "Fine."

He led her to one of the private library rooms on campus. As they went in, Ebony was torn between anger and desire. She wanted to hate him for making her look like a fool. At the same time, she wanted to kiss him so badly she could taste it. But she was silent all through the journey to the room.

"I'm sorry," he began softly. "I just don't want it to look like I'm taking advantage of you." Ebony was confused. "What do you mean?" she asked.

"The thing is, I find you very attractive. You have grown into an amazing woman, and I'd be lying if I said I don't want to be with you."

"So?" Ebony asked. She wasn't sure if she was angry, confused, or indifferent about his reaction.

"I don't know," Sean told her. "I just can't put it into words."

"Kiss me," Ebony commanded him. "Kiss me like you mean it."

He hesitated initially, but Ebony exploded from within when their lips met. She managed to draw down the window shutters before leaning into him. His arms held her close, pressing her breasts to his chest.

"Wait," he said hoarsely as he broke the kiss. "Are you sure about this?"

Ebony didn't reply. Instead, she kissed him deeper, running her fingers along the lines of his arms. Sean reacted, bringing her closer for a deeper kiss. He pinned her hands against the wall with one hand and managed to unhook a bra with the other. He let go of her hands, and Ebony helped him with her shirt, tugging quickly at his afterward. They stood before each other, naked from the waist up.

"My goodness! You're beautiful," Sean said as he caressed one of her breasts.

"Take me," she whispered into his ear.

He obeyed her like a lamb, trailing soft kisses from her lips to her neck and over each breast. Then he took a nipple, biting down on it softly. Ebony found his bulge and rubbed it slowly, responding to the rhythm of his kisses on her breast. She found the zipper and freed him before rubbing his dick over her thighs.

Sean grunted softly, led on by mad desire. He worked his way under her skirt and hastily tore her panties.

"Oh," he said, chuckling.

"Don't stop," Ebony told him,

He made her lean backward and trailed his kisses over her abdomen till he was in the fold between her legs. His first kiss sent her crashing into a whirlpool of pleasure. The second kiss was soft, but Ebony felt like someone had turned on a tap, leaving it open as pleasure coursed through her recklessly. She wanted him deep inside her before she lost her mind.

"Please, take me," she pleaded. "Please."

He raised his head and saw her eyes through the haze in his. He knew he had to give her what she wanted. Slowly, he entered her, numbing her senses. He jerked hard, hitting the walls of her womanhood.

"Yes," Ebony moaned. "Harder."

He rammed into her again, shuddering as passion ran through his body like liquid fire. They managed to keep their moans only for each other's ears, whispering promises of a future they would share. Ebony held on as he continued to tear down every doubt she had about this. When he finally exploded deep inside her, she felt the stars within her reach. She knew she was in the room with him, but she was far away, where nothing else mattered but this moment. She had finally found the rhythm of her songs.

2

SHANICE AND BRYAN

BY CYNTHIA STAR

The night was dark and breezy, and I was about five chapters into the book in my hand. I wasn't particularly liking it, but I couldn't just toss and turn all night, now could I? Maybe that was the better option, I thought to myself as I closed the book, flicked off the lamp, and lay on the bed, hoping the breeze would take me into dreams. Bryan was lying on the bed next to me, perhaps sleeping, I couldn't tell. His face was turned to the other side. His back to me, just like every other night.

I wrapped my arms around him. Instantly, he stiffened. *Guess he's awake then.*

It wasn't always like this. Bryan and I used to be a much better couple. We used to be young and in love. We were still in love, but well, as the saying goes, "romance dies."

Back then, when I was ready to sleep after reading late into the night, I would slip my arm around him, and he would turn to face me fully and kiss me, pulling me close to him...longing for me.

He would pull off my thin nightwear to discover that I had no panties on and mutter, "You silly" before leading me to give him a blowjob, and then sex.

Back then, we made love more than memories. The minute we walked into an empty room, public or private, we would dive at each other's throats, completely devouring each other.

That was back then. These days, nothing was the same anymore.

After ten years of marriage, perhaps it is only natural for the thrill to take a leave of absence.

I let my arm linger for a bit before I moved away and turned to face the other side with a familiar sadness in my heart.

I was desperate, willing to do anything to win back Bryan, to make it right between us. I sat up and folded my arms across my chest. To hell with dreamland. I wasn't sleepy, anyway.

"Bryan," I called, knowing for a fact now that he was awake.

He turned.

"The last few months have been hell for me. How has it been for you?"

"Damn good," he muttered. I couldn't see his eyes in the dim moonlight, but his tone suggested that he was not worried like I was.

He should have seen my eyes widen in shock and amusement. "I'm sure you aren't cheating on me, Bryan, are you?" I asked, dreading what his response might be.

"Of course not, Shanice. You know I love you." By now, he had sat up too, sitting shoulder to shoulder with me.

I heaved a sigh of relief and asked in a calmer voice, "How do you get off then?"

He was quiet for a while. I could hear the sound of his breath as it rose and fell. "You really want to know?"

I nodded, staring at him, anticipating a response like sex toys or porn, but what he said put me off guard, nothing like I had anticipated.

"I get turned on by women who take control of men."

For many minutes, I stared at his face in the dim light in amazement. My silence seemed to indicate my approval, and so he continued, "I have seen a lot of fucking videos of female doms and their sissies. I want to be your sub. Would you be my dom, Shanice?" His statement blew me away. Bryan, the fucking stud, had just asked me to dominate him???

"Let's give it some time, Bryan. I'll need to look before I leap," I said, hesitating at each word. I was frightened to say no, afraid to lose my husband but at the same time exhilarated by the thought of being in control.

Bryan slipped back to sleep beside me. His soft snores soon filled the room, punctuating my thoughts at intervals.

The day dawned quickly. I'd barely closed my eyes when I heard the sound of the bedside alarm announcing that it was 5:30 a.m. Bryan was still sleeping soundly beside me. His day usually started about an hour after mine. He would come to the living room fully dressed for work and demand his breakfast before leaving for work in his truck.

I hopped out of bed, got into my robe, and left the room, heading for the kitchen. There was a spring in my step as I went around the house, arranging the chairs, dusting the counters, and sweeping the floor. Even while I prepared breakfast, our conversation was cooking in my mind. *I get turned on by women who control men.* Bryan's words played in my ears again and again. Before dozing off, I'd made a mental note to read up on that as much as I could as soon as I got to the library–where I worked.

After setting out his breakfast in Bryan's spot, I left to take my bath and get ready for work.

Bryan was not in bed when I got into the bedroom. I didn't hear him in the shower either, but the door to his closet was shut.

I pulled off my nightie, leaving on only my panties

and bra, and went into the bathroom. In a short time, I was done.

Prior to getting into my dress, I took a moment to admire myself in the mirror, tracing each part as I looked at them: my large, perky breasts, my thin waist and fully curved hips; my long white and smooth legs. I needed to cut my toenails and shave, and I sure as hell needed a break. All of a sudden, I wanted to be treated like a queen. Bryan was at the dining table when I got there to join him for breakfast as usual.

"Good morning, lovely," he greeted, taking my hand up to his mouth to kiss it and then lick it.

I could feel his wet tongue on my fingers, going up my hand. I shifted backwards in a jerk, almost hitting his jaw, recalling his words from earlier. He smiled and returned to his meal. He was serious; he wanted me to be in control. Even though my mind wanted to protest, I was ready to take up the challenge. Anything for my marriage.

"I sent an email this morning asking to get out early today," he said.

I wanted to scream, "What the heck?" but I sat down to eat and didn't say much else till he left for work.

"I will take the bus. You take the truck. Have a nice day. I love you, Shanice!" he said before leaving.

I didn't utter a response, but his last sentence kept ringing in my head as I strode out of the front door and began walking, refusing to take the truck.

The day was bright. On the way, I saw a car with a half-opened door on a dark street. At first, I wondered if it was some kind of emergency, but when I peeked inside, I saw a woman writhing with her head thrown back in pleasure in the passenger's seat. There was a man kneeling between her legs with his head down.

She pulled on his hair, and he lifted his face, which was covered in cum. As soon as she had allowed him to have enough air, she shoved him down again. Soon she was screaming and saying, "Fuck! Fuck! Lick up all of it, baby boy!"

I couldn't take it anymore. It made me want to take the woman's place, to feel what she was feeling and scream what she was moaning. It made me want to hurry home and ask Bryan for the same. I hastened my steps; the library where I worked was just a stone's throw from where I was.

The first thing I did when I got into the library was go to the section for books on BDSM and fem dom. There were a number of them, a lot of them actually. I chose one with the title *Domination and Submission* and another on BDSM and hurried to my table to settle into a rigorous read.

For many hours, I was engaged, glancing between the two, reading and looking up pictures. The more I read and saw, and the more excited I became. The whole idea didn't sound strange or absurd to me anymore; instead, it made me wet and caused my nipples to harden.

I wanted to be a mistress; I was ready to take my place as Mistress Shanice.

Many ideas ran through my head of what I would do to/with Bryan this Saturday, but first I had to shop for some mistress and sissy clothes. I returned one of the books to the shelf and tucked the other into my handbag, walked to the counter, and said to my assistant librarian, "Can you fill in for me? I have a terrible headache."

Without waiting for me to say more, she nodded eagerly in affirmation. She was a newly graduated college student who had always wanted to fill in my absence, to handle the readers that came by, and now was her chance to shine. I told her goodbye and struggled to keep a straight face as I went out the door, headed for the mall.

I pulled out my phone and sent Bryan a message that read:

Hey Sissy!

He replied with a grinning emoji.

I wanted to text back something like, *Are you a horse? Cuz I want you in my stable this weekend.*

Instead I sent, *Good boy!* with a poop emoji and laughed, putting my phone back in my handbag.

I wasn't going to tell him what I had in mind just yet, that he was no longer going to call me Shanice or lovely; my new name was Mistress. And that I was heading to the mall to get us both new outfits.

At the mall, I went to the lingerie section first and mused over the mannequins and dresses. They all looked like superheroes in different lingerie. I was intrigued by one of the mannequins in a black silk and lace corset, with matching fishnet stockings that came mid-thigh. I imagined myself in the open, see-through costume. It would reveal my hot curves perfectly and expose my cleavage in a sexually appealing way, a way that would make Bryan hard as a rock.

Leather gloves would be on my hands, a black thin whip in my right and a silver handcuff dangling from the other. I mused over it one more time, feeling myself get even wetter at the thought of wearing that outfit. I put it in my shopping basket and went on to get a pair of handcuffs, a sex collar with a large ring in the front, a whip, a rope, and a paddle.

I heard Bryan talking loudly over the phone when I got to the front door of our house. A smile played on my lips as I reimagined my plans for the weekend. He turned when I pushed the door open and waved at me with a smile, telling me with gestures that he was speaking to a client.

The floors were mopped clean and the furniture shone, I noticed.

After dropping my shopping bag in the bedroom, I went to the kitchen to have a drink. It was scrubbed clean. The dishes were no longer in the sink but washed, wiped dry, and put away. I almost burst into a belly laugh as I imagined him doing all the chores I used to do.

His call was taking too much time. I walked over to him, grabbed the phone from his hand, and disconnected it. He stared at me, surprised, and then tried to reach for it. I raised my hands to put it out of his reach and said, "No more calls. Mistress Shanice needs to talk to you before we do some horsey work."

He grinned, a glint of excitement in his eyes, and said, "Yes, Mistress. Your sub is always at your service."

"Good." I turned off the phone and placed it on a high shelf. "Now stand up!" I ordered.

He obliged, trembling a bit, excited and at the same time anxious, wondering what I would do to him next. I smiled menacingly and walked over to him slowly and seductively. I could see him beginning to tremble with each step I took closer. I stopped in front of him, staring into his eyes— he was one or two inches taller than me, but it didn't matter.

Our noses touched, and our lips almost met; I could feel his heavy breath on my face. His dick was hard against my crotch. Just like I guessed, he thought I wanted to kiss him. Even though I really wanted to, I'd decided to take it slowly. I moved away and said, "We have to talk. Come with me."

We sat at the dining table. I didn't utter a word until he served me whiskey and settled into one of the two chairs on the side. I talked about my research on female-led relationships and said I was interested in leading ours, then we reached an agreement on our likes and dislikes and what was acceptable and unacceptable. Later on, we watched some porn videos of women spanking men and went to sleep. Saturday night was game-on. I'd be one hell of a fucking mistress and save my marriage in the process of climaxing.

I yawned; dawn had come. The night had seemed to go on forever. I lazily opened my eyes. I'd dozed off fantasizing about the plans I had for Bryan, turning them over and over in my head. I glanced at his side, not surprised to see that he was not there. I got up and walked out of the bedroom, hearing him in the kitchen. The table was already set for a meal of bacon and potatoes. I went around and sat at the head of the table. Bryan came out just in time, wearing shorts and a thin singlet that revealed his wide chest, muscles, and hot, hairy legs.

"Good morning, Mistress. I was hoping to serve you in bed. How are you doing this morning?" he asked, setting down two steaming cups of coffee.

"I prefer it here." I picked up a fork to taste the delicious-smelling breakfast, hoping it tasted as good as it smelled. He watched me, desperate for my approval.

It was terrible, tasteless, and half-cooked. I spat it back into the plate, not minding that the rest of the food would be ruined. His face fell; he was trembling,

"I can make something else quickly. Drink the coffee while I do." He was trembling, dreading what would follow.

"This is a bad first impression. The bacon is tasteless; the potatoes are half done! You are not just a sissy but a terrible cook!" I yelled. He pleaded further, shoving the cup of coffee toward me. I pushed it away, spilling some on the floor. With a sweep of my hand, I waved him off and wiped my mouth.

He stood and watched me; his face was flushed to a bright red. It made me horny, made me want to kiss him.

"Face the damn wall and remain that way till I return!" I pointed to the wall, pretending to be angry.

He nodded and went over to the side of the room, trembling even more.

"I am going to teach you a lesson that will stay with you for a long time," I said. "Take off all your clothes before I get back." I walked into the bedroom.

I needed to have a hot bath.

After spanking him, he would suck my pussy just the way I liked it. I went to the tub, undressed, and slid in. I took my time to wash myself thoroughly then pulled out a razor and shaved my legs. I shaved my pussy as well, ensuring that not one hair was missed so it would be as smooth as a baby's bottom. Finally, I got out of the tub, dried off, and went to the bedroom. The bag I had brought from the mall was in a corner of my closet, oblivious to Bryan's eyes.

I took Bryan's favorite perfume and squirted some on my neck, between my breasts, and on my wrists as I rubbed them together. I spent time applying my makeup perfectly like I was going out to an expensive restaurant or somewhere special. Then I pulled out the lingerie outfit from the bag. The black silk and lace corset was difficult to put on alone, but I managed. The corset pushed my tits up high so they were on display for his viewing pleasure. I made sure the stockings were on straight and the clips were perfectly in line with my thighs. The outfit looked more beautiful than I had imagined it would be at the mall.

"You're taking forever in there, Mistress. What are you doing?" Bryan complained in a soft, seductive voice.

"You don't speak to your Mistress that way, you nasty boy. You're getting even deeper in trouble. You'd better be facing that wall when I get back down, boy."

Fully dressed with lightweight pieces of jewelry and my gloves, I got into my heels. Before leaving the room, I took one look at myself in the mirror—admiring how I looked in the outfit—picked up the sex collar, ropes, handcuff, and paddle, and left the room.

Bryan was completely naked, facing the wall, trembling badly. I could see his hot back, his wide shoulders, his triangle shape, his strong build. He heard me approaching and started to turn, but I said in a firm voice, "Don't move yet!"

I got close to him and slipped the sex collar around his neck, then fastened the handcuffs around his hands, behind his back. I grabbed his arm roughly and hurled him to the living room. He groaned in pleasure, muttering some words about loving his mistress. I forced him to his knees facing the empty coffee table, and tied him to the legs. I'd imagined this so much that seeing it happen excited me as much as it excited him.

I turned around to face him and commanded him to look up now. His eyes widened in surprise and ecstasy. He looked at me in admiration. His cock was rock hard and hungry to fuck my brains out. His eyes lit up with excitement, and he tugged at the cuffs and ropes; he wanted to be released. I smiled menacingly and picked the paddle from the chair where I had put it while I tied the ropes.

"You have been a bad boy, and you will pay for it," I said, sounding furious, even though I was really not angry. "What are you?" I swung the paddle and landed it on his ass.

"I am a sub, a slave." He groaned and closed his eyes tightly.

"I can't hear you!" I hit him harder.

"I am a worthless slave and slut. I am forever your sub," he whimpered.

"One that would do anything for his mistress?"

"Um yes, to suck her nipples, to suck her till she screams. I am your slave."

"I like that." I laughed before spanking him again. "Now for your complaining." I lifted the paddle as high as my hand would go and slammed it down on his ass.

"Arghhh, yes, Mistress." His ass was red, with imprints of the paddle. I dropped the toy and sat on the table, my legs on each side of him.

I released the clips from my garter belt, pulled off my panties, threw them in his face, and said, "Suck me without your hands till I scream—just the way I want. Mistress Shanice wanna see the stuff her sub is made of."

He lowered his head to my pussy and sniffed. My pussy was wet and hungry, wanting an orgasm, crying to be touched by his wet tongue. He kissed my labia, nibbling on it slowly. A few more nibbles, a few more kisses as he explored around my vagina. He got to my vagina and licked some of my juices. I wanted his tongue on my clit. He tugged at the hand-cuffs, longing to be released, longing to touch me, to feel me with his hands. I moved away and teased him with the sight of my pussy. He was hungry for me.

It aroused me strongly. I slipped my middle digit into my pulsating pussy and fingerfucked myself, moaning and moving my hips slowly. He moaned and tugged at the ropes, wanting to be free. I slipped another finger in and fucked faster. When I felt an orgasm coming, I stopped and pushed my pussy roughly against his face. He tugged at the handcuffs again.

He moved his head back and gave my clit one flick of his tongue. My entire body shook as if I could explode at any moment. I moaned heavily and pushed my pussy against his face deeper. He sucked my pussy like it was the sweetest orange. I reached down to release his hand from the cuffs but left him tied to the table.

"Lick me!"

One of his hands played with my nipples while his hand fucked my vagina, making me scream in pleasure. His tongue moved up each of my pussy lips, occasionally plunging between them and tasting the fluid that was now spilling from me in hot, musky rivulets. He teased the firm bud of my clitoris and sucked the surrounding petals hungrily.

He knew just how to lick me, where to go firm and where to flick lightly. I caressed his head and held him to me. When he increased the pace of his tongue on my clit, I howled and thrust my cunt against his mouth. After a few minutes, I came for the second time and stood up from the table.

"Now it's time to give my loyal sub a treat," I said and lowered my lips to his hard, throbbing cock. I circled my fingers around his dick and moved in a back-and-forth rhythm, leaning in to kiss him on the lips. I liked the feeling of his soft hands and how hard his dick felt in my hand.

He moaned and tugged at the ropes. Now he wanted more than just masturbating each other, but I had planned that for later in the night. I didn't stop. He was soon oozing precum. I lowered to suck it hungrily, moving my mouth up and down the length of him, kissing, licking, and eating, then stopped when I felt his dick grow bigger in mouth. I straightened myself and cuffed his hands behind his back again.

"I will get back to you when I have had a real breakfast," I said and walked away into the kitchen.

This was just the beginning of my dominance, and I was loving every second of it.

GOOD GIRL

BY PATRICE GLENN

Aliyah was a young girl who loved going to church. She was deeply religious and had a humble demeanor that drew people toward her. Her Sundays were spent attending mass, singing hymns, and offering prayers. One Sunday, as she was walking out of the church, she heard a voice call out to her.

"Excuse me, miss. I'm sorry to bother you, but I couldn't help but notice your beautiful voice during the hymns. My name is Ben," said a shy boy with an endearing smile.

Aliyah smiled back, feeling a warmth spread through her heart. They struck up a conversation, and she found herself drawn to his chatterbox personality. Over the next few weeks, they saw each other regularly, and Ben would share his thoughts and ideas with Aliyah, who would listen patiently.

Aliyah found herself falling for Ben's charm and easygoing nature. She saw a kind soul behind his talkative demeanor and began appreciating their time together. They started dating, and for a while, everything was perfect.

But as time went by, they began to notice their differences. Ben's talkative nature could sometimes come across as insensitive, while Aliyah's deep religious beliefs often left him feeling left out. They tried to work through their differences but ultimately realized they were not meant to be together.

It was a tough decision for both of them, but they knew it was right. They parted ways, still fond of each other but with an understanding that they were not compatible. Aliyah continued to attend church and found solace in her faith.

The same story happened with her next boyfriend. He was too caring. The next one was too dominating. The next one was too irritating. Over the next three years, Aliyah dated lots of boys. She always had something to say about them whenever they went their separate ways. But there was one reason behind everything. It was a statement that Aliyah dreaded more than death itself, a foreboding she could never get rid of. Her mother had often warned her about one thing boys loved more than a girl's beautiful body: sex.

Aliyah had never been one to believe in love at first sight, but when she met Sam at college, she knew that he was different. He was tall, with a muscular build that could only come from playing basketball regularly. His bright smile and warm demeanor had a way of making her feel at ease, and she found herself drawn to him in ways she had never experienced before.

They first met at a student organization event, where they had both volunteered to help set up. Sam had been carrying a heavy box of supplies when he accidentally bumped into Aliyah, causing her to spill her drink all over herself. He had been mortified, apologizing profusely and offering to help her clean up.

"I'm so sorry. I wasn't looking where I was going. Let

me help you clean up," he had said, his deep voice laced with concern.

Aliyah had smiled, feeling a warmth spread through her heart. They struck up a conversation, and she found herself laughing at his jokes and stories. They exchanged numbers, and soon enough, they were going on dates regularly.

Their first date was at a cozy restaurant near campus. They talked for hours, sharing stories about their childhoods, their hopes, and their dreams. Sam was a great listener, always knowing when to talk and when not to. Aliyah found herself feeling at ease in his presence, enjoying his company more than she had ever enjoyed anyone's before.

As they walked out of the restaurant, Sam took her hand, looking into her eyes.

"Aliyah, I know it's only our first date, but I feel like I've known you forever. Would you like to go on another date with me?" he asked, his voice soft and earnest.

Aliyah smiled, feeling a flutter in her chest. "I'd love to," she replied.

They went on many more dates after that, from watching movies at the campus theater to playing basketball together at the school gym. Sam was a skilled player, and he taught her a few tricks, making her feel like she was part of the team.

A few days after their first date, they were walking on campus when Aliyah noticed a group of students huddled around something. She walked over to see what was going on and saw Sam in the middle, holding a puppy.

"Look at this little guy! He was abandoned by his owners, so I decided to take him in. I'm thinking of naming him Kobe," he said, his face lighting up with joy.

Aliyah couldn't help but smile, feeling a warmth spread through her heart.

"You're such a softie," she teased, gently patting the puppy's head.

Sam grinned, looking at her.

"You know me too well already," he said, his eyes twinkling with amusement.

As they walked away, Aliyah felt a sense of contentment wash over her. She knew that Sam was
different from anyone she had ever met, and she felt
lucky to have found someone like him.

Over the next few months, their relationship deep-
ened. They discussed their future together, from
where they wanted to live to how many kids they
wanted. Sam was caring and thoughtful, always
surprising her with little gestures of love.

One day, as they were walking on campus, Aliyah
noticed a group of students practicing a dance
routine for an upcoming event. She watched, feeling
a little envious.

"I wish I could dance like that," she said wistfully.

Sam smiled, looking at her.

"I used to be a pretty good dancer back in high
school. Want me to teach you?" he offered.

Aliyah grinned, feeling a flutter in her chest.

"I'd love that," she replied.

They spent the next hour dancing together, with
Sam teaching Aliyah the basic steps. She initially felt
a little awkward, but with Sam's patient guidance,

she started to get the hang of it. They danced to upbeat music, their bodies moving in sync. Aliyah felt a sense of exhilaration, enjoying the feeling of being in Sam's arms.

Sam twirled her around as they finished their dance, bringing her close to him. They were breathing heavily, their eyes locked on to each other.

"You're a natural," Sam said, his voice soft and husky.

Aliyah felt a blush rise to her cheeks, feeling a little shy.

"I had a great teacher," she replied, grateful for Sam's patience and guidance.

Over the next few weeks, they continued to practice dancing together. They found an empty classroom on campus and would spend hours dancing to music, laughing, and enjoying each other's company. Aliyah felt a sense of joy and contentment in Sam's presence, and she knew he felt the same way.

One day, as they were sitting on a bench near the basketball court, Sam took her hand, looking into her eyes.

"Aliyah, we've only been dating for a few months, but I feel like I've known you forever. I want to be with you forever. Will you be my girlfriend?" he asked, his voice soft and earnest.

Aliyah felt a flutter in her chest, tears filling her eyes.

"Yes, Sam. I want to be your girlfriend," she replied, her voice filled with emotion.

Sam leaned in, kissing her gently on the lips. They held each other close, feeling a sense of joy and contentment wash over them. Aliyah was happy. She had thought Sam was no longer interested in taking things higher than their friendship. But now that he had asked her to be his girlfriend, she felt incredibly joyous.

However, their relationship lasted for only a few months. Sam wanted sex. He was very understanding when Aliyah told him she wasn't ready for something like that. He didn't complain or push too hard. Instead, they both agreed she'd give him a hand job anytime he was horny. The first time they did it, Aliyah felt it was very awkward. Sam was gentle, though. He held her close and kissed her softly.

"All you need to do is continue stroking my dick," he told her. "Don't look down there."

And that was precisely what they did. Aliyah rubbed his dick hard. She didn't know how he enjoyed it, but it seemed that he liked what she was doing. He grunted loudly, throwing his head back with short gasps until she felt something sticky on her hands. Sam looked like he was having a fit, and she didn't know what to do.

"Are you okay?" she asked him.

He finally sighed deeply and nodded. Then he hugged her and kissed her passionately. Since then, things went well between them until the day Sam told her he wanted more.

"You can do this," he said to her. "It's not even that hard. Just let me handle things."

But Aliyah refused to do anything other than what she had been doing before. Sam picked up her things in anger and shoved them into her hands, telling her to get out.

"What?!" she asked, bewildered.

"You heard me," he responded. "Get out and never come back here. Don't even think of calling me."

"Are you breaking up with me?" Aliyah asked. Her heart was heavy. "Sam?"

He didn't reply. He just pushed her out of the room and shut the door after her.

As Aliyah stormed out of Sam's room, her heart was heavy with emotion. She couldn't believe that the man she had loved and trusted had just broken up with her over something so trivial.

She had always known that Sam was a little impatient when it came to matters of the heart, but she had hoped that he would understand her desire to wait until the right time. But it seemed that he was more interested in satisfying his desires than respecting her wishes. As she walked through the campus, her mind was filled with thoughts of their relationship. She had thought that they had something special, something that would last forever. But their love seemed to not be strong enough to weather the storm.

As she reached her dorm room, she collapsed onto her bed, tears streaming down her face. She felt lost and alone, wondering how she could ever find love again after this heartbreak. Days went by, and she found solace in her faith. She spent time in prayer, asking for guidance and strength to get through this difficult time. She also contacted her Christian friends, who offered their support and comfort.

As time passed, she realized that she had grown stronger and more resilient. She knew that she deserved someone who respected her and loved her for who she was, not just for what she could offer physically. And so she moved on from Sam, knowing that she deserved someone who shared her values and respected her boundaries. She continued to go to church, finding comfort in the teachings of her faith.

It had been years since Aliyah had decided she wouldn't let her guard down around any man. After the incident with Sam, she decided she wanted more in life than what men were offering her. She got a job as a kindergarten teacher after she finished school, which she loved. Every day, she would walk into her classroom with a big smile on her face, ready to greet her students with open arms. And the kids loved her just as much, always eager to learn and play with her. She had always loved children, and teaching had been her dream ever since she was a little girl. And now, she was living that dream, helping to shape the minds and hearts of the next generation.

She loved watching her students grow and learn, seeing the wonder and curiosity in their eyes as they discovered new things about the world around them. And she loved being able to nurture and care for them, to be a positive influence in their lives.

One of her favorite things to do with her students was to read them stories. She had a whole collection of children's books, from classic fairy tales to modern picture books. And the kids would sit around her in a circle, their eyes glued to the pages as she read aloud in her gentle, soothing voice.

She also loved to sing with her students, teaching them nursery rhymes and songs that they could sing together. And they would often have dance parties, moving and grooving to their favorite tunes.

But there was one thing Aliyah loved more than all these things. She had tried to hide it from the first day, but with each passing moment, it got harder for her to deny it. It was the assistant principal. He was funny, jovial, outspoken, and very kind-hearted. Of course, she kept her feelings to herself since she knew he might not like her the same way.

Aliyah had been crushing on Roberts for weeks now, but he was about to leave for a new job in another state. She couldn't believe that she was never going to see him again, and her heart ached at the thought.

Aliyah knew she couldn't tell him how she felt. That would be unprofessional, and she didn't want to risk her job or her reputation. So she admired him from afar, watching him as he moved through the hallways with grace and authority.

And then, one day, he surprised her. It was the day before he was due to leave, and they were all going out for a drink. Aliyah was nervous, not knowing what to expect. She had never been out drinking with her colleagues before, and she didn't want to embarrass herself in front of Roberts.

But as the night wore on, she found herself loosening up, laughing and joking with her coworkers. And then, out of nowhere, Roberts started hitting on her.

At first, she was taken aback, not knowing how to respond. But then she started to feel a flutter in her stomach, a warm, tingling sensation that spread through her body. She realized that she was actually enjoying the attention that she had been craving for so long.

Roberts was charming and funny, and he had a way of making her feel special. He listened to her stories, asked her questions about her life, and laughed at her jokes. And Aliyah found herself drawn to him like a moth to a flame.

They drank and talked for hours, their conversation ranging from silly to serious. They discussed their dreams and aspirations, their hopes and fears. And Aliyah found herself opening up to him in ways that she never had before.

And then, as the night wore on, Roberts leaned in and whispered in her ear, "I've been wanting to do this all night." And then he planted a soft kiss on her lips.

Aliyah was shocked, but she didn't pull away. Instead, she leaned into him, her heart racing with excitement. She knew that this was wrong, that she shouldn't be doing this, but she couldn't help herself.

They kissed for a while, their passion growing with each passing moment. And then, Roberts pulled away, his eyes locked on to hers.

Aliyah couldn't believe that the man she had been crushing on for so long had just kissed her. She was confused and didn't know how to react, but Roberts didn't give her much time to think as he began to speak.

"I know this might seem sudden, but I've had feelings for you for a while now," he said, his voice low and full of sincerity. "I see the way you look at me, and I can't help but feel drawn to you."

Aliyah's heart skipped a beat at his words. She had always thought that he was out of her league, and the fact that he had feelings for her was over-whelming.

"I-I don't know what to say," she stuttered, feeling flustered.

"It's okay, Aliyah," Roberts said reassuringly, taking her hand in his. "I don't want to pressure you into anything, but I just had to tell you how I feel. I understand if you need time to process this."

Aliyah nodded, feeling grateful for his understanding. They continued to talk for a while, and she found herself opening up to him about her past relationships and her fears of getting hurt again.

Roberts listened attentively, offering words of comfort and encouragement. He was patient and kind, and Aliyah felt safe in his presence.

As the night wore on, the other teachers began to leave the bar one by one until it was just Aliyah and Roberts. They were feeling a little tipsy and didn't want the night to end.

"I don't want to say goodbye," Roberts said, looking at Aliyah with a twinkle in his eye. "Why don't we go back to my place? It's just around the corner, and we can have a few more drinks."

Aliyah hesitated for a moment, but something inside her told her to take a chance. She nodded her head, and they left the bar, hand in hand.

As they walked down the quiet street, Roberts spoke softly to her, telling her how beautiful she looked and how much he had enjoyed their conversation.

Aliyah blushed, feeling like a schoolgirl with a crush.

When they arrived at Roberts' house, Aliyah was a bit nervous, but Roberts did his best to put her at ease. He offered her a seat on the couch and went to the kitchen to get some drinks.

They sat down on the couch, and Roberts turned on some soft music. He looked at her and said, "You know, Aliyah, I really like you. I've been wanting to tell you for a while now."

Aliyah smiled shyly and said, "I like you too, Roberts."

He moved closer, and she felt her heart start to race. He gently took her hand and looked into her eyes. "Aliyah, I know we don't know each other that well, but I feel like we have a connection. I want to get to know you better."

Aliyah felt a jolt of electricity shoot through her body at his touch. "I want to get to know you better too, Roberts," she said softly.

They sat there in silence for a moment, enjoying each other's company. Roberts then leaned in and kissed her. It was a soft, gentle kiss, and Aliyah felt herself melting into his arms.

They continued kissing for a while, and Aliyah began to feel more comfortable around him. She had never felt this way before, and it scared her a little, but she also felt alive and happy.

"Roberts," she said, breaking the kiss, "I don't know what this means for us. I don't want to rush things."

Roberts smiled and took her hand. "Aliyah, I understand. We can take things slowly, and we don't have to rush into anything. I just want to be with you, and I want to make you happy."

Before Aliyah knew it, the night had flown by, and it was well past midnight. She looked at Roberts and saw the desire in his eyes. He leaned in to kiss her again.

"You're still resisting," he said softly.

Aliyah smiled.

"Here, feel my dick," he said to her.

Aliyah gasped softly. She didn't know a man could be packing this much. His dick was thrice the size of any man she had ever been with. Something in her snapped, and she just wanted to feel this inside her.

A part of her felt guilty for ignoring her mother's warnings about sex. But she was a grown woman now. She didn't want to keep living in the past and lose her chance to fall in love again.

Aliyah also remembered she had told herself she wouldn't play into any man's hands anymore. But she wanted this to happen. Maybe she was going to regret it in the morning, but right now, she wanted him deep inside her.

Roberts leaned in and kissed her again. The kiss was soft and gentle at first, but it became more passionate. Aliyah felt her body respond to his touch, knowing she wanted him as much as he wanted her.

They moved to the bedroom, shedding their clothes as they went. Roberts was a considerate lover, making sure that Aliyah felt comfortable and cared for every step of the way. He helped her out of her clothes and gazed at her body for a while. Aliyah wanted to cover herself up, but he held her hands instead.

"You're more beautiful than anything I've ever seen in my life," he said softly.

Aliyah blushed lightly. "There is something I need to tell you, though," she said quickly.

"What's that?" Roberts asked. He had pulled his trousers off already.

"I'm a virgin," she said shyly.

Roberts sighed. He placed a hand on her shoulder and gave it a light squeeze.

"It's okay. I know," he said. "And I promise you, I'll be very gentle."

Aliyah sighed and nodded. She had come this far, and it would be stupid to quit now. She let Roberts draw her closer and collapsed against him. The kiss was tender this time around, but it also felt soothing. He was very good with his hands, exploring every inch of her body. Aliyah squirmed and sighed, desperate for a want she had never known before. Roberts kissed her belly and traced the kiss up to her neck. She jerked, unable to contain the pleasures threatening to tear her into shreds. Finally, he let her touch his dick again, and it felt huge and warm in her hand. She stroked him gently, craving it inside her instead. Unable to keep herself under control, she pushed him back and got on top of him.

Before Roberts could stop her, she slid his bulge into her center.

The pain that surged through her was unlike anything Aliyah had ever felt before. It numbed her senses for a while, and she felt her head spin. But shortly after that, a new wave of pleasure enveloped her totally. It drove her mad, and in an instant, she was a beast filled with instincts. She rode him like he was a horse, laughing and crying at the same time as waves of pleasure crashed over her. When she finally reached the peak, she collapsed against him and kept riding until she lost herself in him completely.

Roberts managed to hold on to her until he also came. She fell against him and immediately fell asleep. There was a tiny stain of red on the sheets, but that could wait. Right now, holding Aliyah was all that mattered.

4

———

ANAL PLUNGE

BY C.C. ELIZABETH

Imani had known Duane since they were both kids. After college, they had both decided to settle in the same area so they could keep in touch. Duane was a handsome young man. He had dreads that were so long they touched the middle of his back. His eyes were perfectly etched in their sockets, a hue of black and brown.

He had a limp from an accident when he was sixteen. He had been driving his dad's car when someone ran into the road unexpectedly. Duane was young, and there was nothing he could have done to stop the car on time. He broke his right leg, and the other person was in a coma for a few weeks. After the incident, Duane found it very hard to walk properly. So instead of feeling sorry for himself, he managed to turn his limp into a walking gait. And that was why Imani liked him more.

When they both turned twenty-one, Duane asked Imani out, but she refused. She told him he was more like a brother to her; a friend she could count on anytime. She didn't want to spoil that friendship by taking things a little too far.

Duane loved Imani more than anything in the world. He dreamt about her dark, full hair and her oval-shaped face each night. He saw her ebony skin in his imagination. Anytime he was lucky enough to touch her, the feeling lingered more than any other thing in the world. For him, she was God's perfect creation. So when she turned him down, he didn't get jealous or bitter. He just decided to be the best friend she'd ever had.

A few months after they'd both started their first jobs, Imani told Duane she wanted to quit. She told him she wanted to try things on her own. She was done working for people who didn't value her expertise.

"So what do you want to do?" Duane asked.

Imani placed her PC on the bed beside her. She had a few ideas, but she wasn't so sure.

"Well, I can freelance," she told him.

"What do you mean?" Duane asked.

Imani turned toward him.

"You know how I love to write, right? So, there are platforms where I can write and get paid for my skills."

Imani waited for him to say something. Before telling him, she had thought about it. There was no need to keep toiling away while some people who did less than what she was doing earned more. Besides, this was something she would enjoy doing. It was a passion.

"You're right," Duane said after a brief moment of silence. "I think you deserve more than you currently earn."

Imani smiled at Duane's words. She appreciated his support and encouragement. She knew she could count on him to always have her back.

Over the next few weeks, Imani researched different freelance writing platforms and started submitting her work. It wasn't easy at first, but she was deter-mined to make it work. She spent long hours at her computer, writing and editing until her fingers were sore.

Duane watched Imani work tirelessly, impressed by her dedication and commitment to her craft. He knew how much she loved to write, and he was happy to see her pursue her passion.

One day, Imani received an email from a popular online magazine. They were interested in publishing one of her articles and offering her a paid contract. Imani was over the moon with excitement. She couldn't believe that her hard work was finally paying off.

Duane was ecstatic for her. He knew how much this meant to her and how hard she had worked to get here. He couldn't be prouder of his best friend.

As Imani continued to write and grow her freelance career, Duane was always there to support her. He helped her with editing, offered feedback, and even assisted in setting up her own website.

Months passed, and Imani became a successful free-lance writer, with her work published in numerous publications. Duane remained her biggest supporter, cheering her on every step of the way.

One day, as they were sitting at a café, Imani turned to Duane with a big smile on her face.

"Do you remember when you asked me out in college?" she asked.

Duane chuckled. "Of course. How could I forget?"

Imani went silent for a minute. Duane could tell she was thinking very hard about something. He prayed it would be something he had wanted all his life.

"So?" he asked quizzically.

Imani smiled a bit.

"I don't know, Duane," she started. "You are a nice guy and everything, and you've always been there for me all my life. I am not sure a relationship would work between us, and that was why I refused your advances back then."

Duane's heart sank. He had thought she was going to finally give him a chance.

"But," Imani continued, "there's something we can do."

Duane's attention was piqued. He leaned forward and asked her what she had in mind.

"I want us to be friends with benefits," she said quickly.

Duane's heart sank as Imani's words registered in his mind. He couldn't believe what he was hearing. He had thought everything was going great between them. He couldn't imagine just being friends with benefits.

"Imani, I don't think that's a good idea," he said, trying to keep his voice calm.

Imani looked at him, surprised. "Why not? We're both adults, and we're not committed to anyone else. It could be fun."

Duane sighed, shaking his head. "I don't think it's that simple. I care about you. I don't want to just use you for sex and then go back to being friends. I want something more than that."

Imani looked at him, a bit hurt. "I understand, Duane, but I don't want anything serious right now. I just want to have some fun and explore my sexuality."

Duane took a deep breath, trying to find the right words.

"I understand that, Imani, but I don't think I'm the right person for that. I don't want to do something that might ruin what we have, and I don't want to risk getting hurt."

Imani looked away, feeling disappointed. She had hoped that Duane would be open to the idea, but now she could see that it wasn't going to happen.

"I understand," she said, her voice barely above a whisper.

For days, Duane couldn't stop thinking about Imani and the offer she had made to him. He knew he had hurt her by refusing, and he didn't want to lose her as a friend or potential partner. As he thought more about it, he started to realize that maybe a friends with benefits situation could work for them.

He reached out to Imani and asked if they could talk about it. When they met, Duane apologized for how he had reacted before and explained that he had been scared of risking their friendship. He told her that he had thought about it more and was willing to give it a try.

Imani was surprised but happy to hear this. She explained that she had felt rejected and hurt by his initial refusal, but that she also understood his concerns. She was willing to give it a try as well, as long as they were both clear about their intentions and boundaries.

And so they began a new phase in their relationship. They agreed to see each other once a week, and to be honest and open about their feelings and desires. They also agreed to keep their arrangement discreet and to respect each other's privacy.

As they explored their physical connection, they also found that their emotional connection grew stronger. They talked more, shared more, and grew closer than ever before. They realized that their friendship had evolved into something deeper and more meaningful.

It so happened that Duane was great in bed. He was greater than anyone Imani had ever been with before. He never rushed. Most times, he liked to kiss her passionately, working his way from her lips to her large tits and down to her belly. His kisses were mostly soft and accompanied with little moans.

Imani was at first afraid he wouldn't know how to give head since she had known him all his life and he'd never talked about it. But Duane beat her imagination. He kissed her inner thighs slowly, lingering between each kiss so she'd gasp and call out his name. Then, he would lay her back gently, working his way from her thigh to her honeypot. His first kiss would jolt her awake, sending her spiraling into an ocean of desires. He would touch her clit softly at first, asking her if she was ready for him.

"Yes, Daddy," Imani would reply, surprised that she could be so vulnerable around him.

Duane liked to suck first. He'd lick the drip that flowed from her slowly, running his tongue down the length of her clit. Then, he'd tease her labia quickly, causing Imani to cry softly. Afterwards, he'd lick her from the inside out. And back again. Then, he'd hold out her clit and slurp until she squirted all over his face. Of course, he'd continue until she was entirely drained. For Imani, sex was always having Duane in control. He was her guide through anything. And he knew all the routes to her pleasure house.

Imani and Duane continued spending more and more time together, both in their friends with benefits arrangement and outside of it. One night, they decided to catch a movie together. As they settled into their seats, Imani couldn't help but feel a little nervous. She had been developing strong feelings for Duane, and she wasn't sure where their relationship was headed.

As the movie began, Imani leaned her head on Duane's shoulder and let out a contented sigh. She felt safe and comfortable with him, and she knew he felt the same way. But as the movie went on, Imani started to feel the urge to use the restroom.

"I'll be right back," she whispered to Duane before getting up and making her way to the restroom.

As she walked down the darkened hallway, Imani heard a voice behind her.

"Hey, handsome. You're here alone?"

She turned around to see a beautiful girl with long, curly hair and a seductive smile.

"Uh, no. I'm actually here with someone," Duane replied, slightly taken aback by the sudden attention.

"Oh, too bad. I was hoping we could watch the movie together," the girl purred.

Duane felt a little uncomfortable, but he didn't want to be rude.

"Sorry, maybe another time," he said, before making his way to the bathroom too since he was a bit pressed.

When Duane returned to their seats, he noticed that Imani looked a little upset. "What's wrong?" he asked, concerned.

"Nothing," Imani replied, trying to hide her jealousy. "Just got lost in my thoughts for a bit."

But Duane could sense that something was bothering her. He gently took her hand in his and looked into her eyes. "Hey, it's just you and me tonight. Nothing else matters," he said, trying to reassure her.

Imani smiled weakly and leaned her head back on his shoulder. But her mind was still racing. She couldn't help but wonder if Duane had been tempted by the other girl's attention.

As the movie came to an end, Duane suggested they grab a drink at a nearby bar. Imani agreed, hoping that a change of scenery would help ease her anxiety.

As they sat at the bar, sipping their drinks, Duane noticed that Imani seemed distant.

"Is everything okay?" he asked.

Imani took a deep breath before speaking. "I saw that girl hitting on you earlier. I couldn't help feeling jealous," she admitted, looking down at her drink.

Duane's heart sank. He had no idea that his brief interaction with the other girl had caused Imani so much distress.

"Imani, there's nothing to be jealous about," he said, trying to reassure her. "I only have eyes for you."

Imani looked up at him, her eyes searching his face for any signs of deception. But all she saw was love and honesty. She smiled, feeling a weight lift off her chest.

"I'm sorry. I guess I'm just being silly," she said, taking a sip of her drink.

Duane took her hand in his and gave it a gentle squeeze.

"You're not being silly. I understand why you would feel that way. But I promise you, you have nothing to worry about."

They continued to talk and laugh, enjoying each other's company. As the night wore on, Imani realized that her feelings for Duane were only getting stronger. She knew that she wanted to be more than just friends with benefits, but she couldn't say anything. This had been her idea, and she'd have to live with the consequences.

A few weeks had passed since the incident at the movies, and Duane had all but forgotten about the girl who had tried to hit on him. But fate had other plans.

One afternoon, while running some errands, Duane found himself face to face with the very same girl. She was standing in front of a coffee shop, looking just as alluring as she had the first time they had met.

Duane felt a twinge of nervousness in his stomach. He wasn't sure how he was supposed to react to her presence. But before he could even make a move, she had already spotted him.

"Hey there, stranger!" she exclaimed, waving enthusiastically at Duane.

Duane tried his best to hide his discomfort.

"Hey," he said cautiously, trying not to make too much eye contact.

The girl seemed undeterred by Duane's awkwardness. She took a step closer to him and leaned in.

"So what brings you to this part of town?"

Duane tried to think of a good excuse to leave, but he found himself tongue-tied.

"Just running some errands," he managed to say.

The girl smiled flirtatiously. "Well, I was just about to grab a coffee. Do you want to join me?"

Duane hesitated for a moment before responding. He wasn't sure if he should accept her offer or politely decline. But before he could make a decision, the girl had already grabbed his hand and started leading him into the coffee shop.

Duane felt his heart rate increase as they walked inside. The girl ordered a coffee for herself and asked Duane if he wanted anything. He declined, trying to come up with an excuse to leave as soon as possible.

But as they waited for the girl's coffee to be made, Duane found himself lost in thought. He couldn't help but feel an attraction toward her. She was beautiful, confident, and seemed to genuinely enjoy his company.

As they sat down at a table, the girl leaned in close to Duane.

"You know, I've been thinking about you since we last met," she said, running her fingers through her hair.

Duane felt a surge of excitement in his chest. He had to remind himself that he was already involved with Imani. But as the girl continued to flirt with him, he found it harder and harder to resist her advances.

Just then, his phone rang. It was Imani. He quickly answered, hoping to avoid any suspicion.

"Hey, what's up?" he said, trying to sound casual.

Imani's voice sounded distant over the phone. "Hey, I just wanted to check in on you. How's your day going?"

Duane glanced over at the girl, who was now scrolling through her phone.

"It's going well. Just running some errands," he said.

Imani paused for a moment. "Is everything okay? You sound a little off."

Duane could feel his heart pounding in his chest. He wasn't sure if Imani was picking up on anything, but he knew he had to play it cool. "Yeah, everything's fine. Just a little tired, I guess," he said.

Imani didn't seem entirely convinced, but she didn't push the issue. "Okay, well, call me later if you need anything," she said.

Duane breathed a sigh of relief as he hung up the phone. He turned back to the girl, who was now looking at him expectantly.

"So what do you say we get out of here?" she said, a sly grin spreading across her face.

Duane chuckled nervously. He knew there was a problem the moment she had forced him to sit with her.

"I honestly don't think that's a good idea," he said slowly. "I mean, you barely even know me."

The girl got out of her seat and came to sit near him. She had her boobs in his face and her hand on his lap.

"Come on. Don't you want some of this?" she asked, rubbing her other hand over her chest.

Duane swallowed hard. He was in a real dilemma now. He had to find a way to get out.

"I'll let you fuck my asshole," the girl said suddenly.

Duane decided he had had enough. It was time for him to leave. He brushed her aside calmly and made his way out of the shop. The girl kept calling after him, but he didn't turn until he was out of sight.

Duane walked into his apartment and immediately picked up his phone to call Imani. He needed to tell her what had happened. He dialed her number and waited patiently as it rang. After a few rings, she picked up.

"Hey, Duane," Imani said in a low voice.

"Hey, Imani. Can you come over? I need to talk to you about something," Duane said, his voice sounding serious.

"Sure, I can be there in twenty minutes," Imani replied.

"Thanks, I'll see you then," Duane said before hanging up.

Duane sat on his couch, his thoughts running wild. He couldn't believe what had just happened. He couldn't believe the girl from the movies was hitting on him again after he had made it clear that he was not interested. He didn't know how to handle the situation, so he needed Imani's help.

Twenty minutes later, Imani arrived at Duane's apartment. He let her in, and they sat down on the couch together.

"So what happened?" Imani asked, looking at Duane with concern.

"Well, I was out running errands, and I ran into that girl from the movies again. She tried to get me to go home with her, but I refused," Duane explained.

Imani's face immediately showed a hint of jealousy. "Why did she want you to go home with her?" she asked, her voice tight.

"I don't know. She said something about wanting to spend more time with me, but I told her I wasn't interested," Duane replied, hoping to calm Imani's jealousy. "She even offered to let me fuck her in the asshole if I wanted. Imagine how crazy that sounds!"

"I can't believe she had the audacity to hit on you after what happened at the movies," Imani fumed.

Duane could see that Imani was still jealous and upset, and he didn't know how to make her feel better. He took her hand in his and looked at her deeply.

"Imani, please don't be jealous. You know how much you mean to me," he said, trying to reassure her.

"I know, but it's hard. I don't want to lose you," Imani said, tears threatening to fall from her eyes.

"You won't lose me, Imani. I care about you too much. You're my best friend, and you always will be," Duane said, pulling Imani into a hug.

Imani hugged him back tightly, feeling comforted by his words. She knew deep down that Duane cared about her, but sometimes, her jealousy got the best of her.

After a few minutes, they pulled away from each other, and Duane spoke again.

"Imani, I want to make something clear. I'm not interested in that girl, or anyone else, for that matter. You're the only one I want to be with," he said, looking at Imani with sincerity.

Imani smiled, feeling happy to hear those words.

"I feel the same way, Duane. I just get jealous sometimes," she admitted.

"It's okay, I understand. Just know that you have nothing to worry about. I'm all yours," Duane said, smiling at her.

Imani smiled back, feeling reassured. Then, her smile got bigger and broader.

"Why are you smiling like that?" Duane asked her.

Imani turned to face him. The smile was still on her face.

"I want to ask you a question and I want you to be sincere with me," she answered.

Duane nodded his head. Imani paused a bit before she continued.

"If you had the opportunity, would you really try anal sex?" she asked.

"Maybe," he replied almost immediately. "It's not that bad. I just can't do it with that girl."

Imani got up and reached into her bag. She got her lube out and walked towards Duane sexily.

"I want you to fuck me in my ass," she said while stripping.

Duane laughed. He thought she was joking at first, but when she moved closer, he realized they were going to really do anal. Imani didn't wait for him to respond, though. She knelt before him and grabbed his dick in her hands. Her mouth came open almost at the same time as she freed his dick from his pants. She sucked him deeply, pushing his shaft all the way down her throat. Then, she slurped and used her hands at the same time. Unable to hold on for long, Duane spilled into her mouth. Imani giggled before swallowing all the juicy cum in her mouth.

"And now for the main event," she said as she grabbed the lube.

At first, they both struggled to get his dick inside properly. But when they managed it, Imani knew the experience was totally worth it. Duane used his dick well, hitting her deeply with each thrust. She reached down and rubbed her clit, enjoying the feeling of being fucked in the ass for the first time ever. The tightness made Duane enjoy it as well. He went harder and faster, increasing his speed with each thrust.

Imani felt her orgasm build slowly, in time with Duane's grunts as he pounded her mercilessly. It felt divine, almost ethereal for her. And when she came, she burst into tears of joy. She could no longer pretend. She wanted him at all costs.

5

THREE

BY RACHAEL WILTON-BLAZE

"Oh shit, baby, don't you fucking stop," Patrice wailed out in pleasure.

Nia, her fiancée, who was standing behind her, bent slightly over her doggy-style position and spanked her ass hard.

"Damn. Baby you're fucking my brains out."

"You like it?" Nia asked without changing rhythm. Back and forth, back and forth, Patrice's wide ass bounced as the bed squealed underneath them.

At that point, Patrice was a few moments away from ecstasy. She rolled her eyes and tilted her head skyward, prior to Nia's hold.

"I said... do you like it?" Nia asked again. This time, she stopped thrusting and grabbed at Patrice's hair so that her ears were just a few inches away from her lips.

"What the fuck, babe? I was just about to cum." Filled with anger and dissatisfaction, Patrice struggled to break out of Nia's hold.

"Damn, baby, it's like that? Come on, don't sweat it, I could easily get you back in sync." Nia talked to her lover, who had broken out of her grasp and pulled her pussy free from the dildo strap.

"Don't bother, we'll get it next time." Patrice sighed and rolled her hair up, panting, out of breath.

Nia walked into the bathroom buck-naked except for the strap she had on, which was bouncing up and down in time with her swift movement. She took it off, making sure to properly clean it before heading back into the room. Patrice was still in the position she'd left her in.

She looked around. The room was a mess. The outfits they'd both had on some minutes earlier were now lying carelessly on the floor of their little bedroom, which was beaming red, due to the bulb they had on.

The necklace she had bought for Patrice on the night they'd gotten engaged lay at the corner of the bed, almost falling off. It took her back to the memory of that night. She'd gotten down on one knee, intent on spending forever with this gorgeous lady.

Patrice, as beautiful as ever, had walked into Nia's apartment that day in a red dress that almost glittered. Nia was standing by the mirror trying to figure out how to tie a knot. A casual dresser, she'd had no use for corporate attire, yet here she found herself in a black tuxedo which looked great on her, but the damn tie was beginning to get on her nerves. It almost had Nia pulling up her dreads. Although they were short, it would make the action even more dramatic.

Nia had a plan. She was going to propose to her girl-friend of two years. She had made a decent living for herself, working online as a top-rated freelancer. She had been killing it these past two years and even had a house she was going to buy in a couple of months.

She already owned a ride, a battered Jeep—not too battered since it still impressed some of the ladies. But she would definitely upgrade to something more befitting. Something that screamed "happily married to a lady; yes, bitches, we're lesbians!"

Nia had always been one for drama, and the night wasn't going to be any different. She had spent an insane amount of time planning for this. Besides her wedding day and perhaps the day she first set her eyes on her kids, this was going to be the most important day of her life. So if she had to get into a damn suit just to look the part, then she would—no questions asked. But to hell with this tie. She was over it.

"You look stunning," Patrice had said as she walked in.

By the time Nia turned to her, she was caught breathless. Patrice looked amazing in that red gown. She was an extremely beautiful woman, 24 at the time.

Her body was the perfect picture of an hourglass with her small waist, large hips—the type you had to make a little hop just to fit into a jeans—and rounded boobs.

The booty was surely no exemption.

The view from the back was just as great as the front, maybe even better—depending on what you preferred. Still, even if you were into boobs, Patrice had that covered as well. Her nipples tugged at the dress, longing to be free just like the corners of her breasts were.

A big lump of meat, soft, moist meat. Who wouldn't eat that?

A grin curved on Nia's face as she traveled yet again down memory lane, back to when she'd first met Patrice in college. Patrice, at that time—not bisexual, came into the club already drunk, crying from a heartbreak. Apparently, she had been dumped by her high school sweetheart who was now miles away from her. Her friends ushered her in, clearing the way for her to pass to get to the bar, right where Nia was seated.

Even with swollen eyes, rumpled clothes, and messy makeup, Patrice still glittered in the eyes of Nia. A simple "hello" could have done it, but the butch lady with a passion for flare handed her drink over to the young lady and said, "If you're going to be crying and drinking, at least take a sip of this."

Patrice who had been feeling the world close in on her earlier, couldn't help but smile briefly, and indeed after she was done drinking from the glass, engrossed in a conversation with Nia, she had forgotten what she was crying about. From that moment on, it was *Goodbye to big, hard cocks* for Patrice to *Welcome Nia, dip your fingers into my pussy till they can go no further.* And more often *Then you can bang my brains out with your strap-on.*

And so it had been, or at least, until then...

"What the hell's happening to us, babe? I'll call it if you won't. We ain't even thirty yet, and it's like this? What the hell's happening to our sex life?" Nia asked, coming out of her thoughts as she sat on the bed beside Patrice.

"I'm tired. Nothing's wrong, we'll go again later. Don't overthink this. I'm tired, that's all."

"Don't give me that, baby; come on, I know you. I know that look. I've been getting it lately. I don't think I'm too old to recognize when a girl's not being satisfied no more." Leaning in, she added, "Is it me? Is it the lack of foreplay and total hardcore? What, the name calling isn't doing it again for you?

Goddammit, talk to me, sweetheart. I'll change whatever."

"You will?" Patrice asked with round baby eyes.

Caught in that look, it was hard not to say yes, and so, Nia responded, "I promise, for you? Anything!"

Certainly she had no way of knowing. There was no way she would have ever thought to hear the next words that came from her girl's lips...

"Do you ever wonder what it would be like?" Patrice asked.

"What what would be like? Come on, ma'am. I'm in no mood for riddles."

"No riddles, just imagination. Don't you ever wonder? I mean, you're a dyke, not entirely a stud. So come on, I'm sure you wonder."

"Wonder what, lady?" Nia replied, growing impatient.

"What it would be... what it would feel like with a man," Patrice finally said.

"Hot damn, baby girl, that's what's got you riled up?

You miss dicks?" Nia said, almost busting out into a belly laugh.

"I don't get what the joke is, and no, I don't miss dicks. I'm asking if you ever wonder what it feels like, considering."

"What? That I've never had dicks?"

"Yes," Patrice murmured under her breath.

It was true; Nia had been a lesbian since birth. Matter of fact, she was damn sure she cried "lesbian" as everyone watched, including the doctor. She had liked boobs the entire time, sucking on her mother's even when she wasn't hungry.

As a little kid, she had liked ass—ladies' ass, specifically her nanny's. The Lord definitely should have caught her multiple times drooling over how big it was and how it would feel to bury her face in it, without fear of the nasty smell that came out of it.

When she was old enough to understand that she came to existence out of the front hole, good Lord, she couldn't wait to go back in there.

She knew she had to; it was her destiny. Even if it was just her pinky, she had to get it in there. And then her mouth, maybe try to fit her entire head in, and when that wouldn't work, she stuck to just the lip, nose, and mouth.

It sure tasted like heaven, and she didn't need any other taste ruining that one for her. So no, Patrice, she'd never thought about a different taste.

"But now that you mention it, I have thought about it once or twice. Mostly out of curiosity, because damn girl, your eyes be rolling real hard for a strap, so a lady's got to imagine the real thing in you, what your reaction would be," she honestly answered. "But I'd rather have it on me than in me."

"Yes, I get it; you're that kind of girl," Patrice said and rolled her eyes.

Before she was able to get up and walk away from the conversation, Nia held her back. "No, baby, we're getting to the root of this. So tell me, you miss dicks, huh? That's what's going on?"

"No, baby, you're enough for me," Patrice replied.

"I know I am, but I'm also aware that sexual cravings and fantasies don't define a person. Just how they'd really like to go down at that moment. So I'll ask again, you miss dicks?"

"Well, before you, all I'd ever had were dicks. The pussy and clit rubbing has been great. Lord knows I'm in heaven when you eat me out, but yes, babe, I miss dicks, and I'm sorry if I've been letting this affect our sexual life." Patrice kept her head down, suddenly seeming more interested in playing with her toenails than looking into the face of her fiancée.

"There's nothing to be sorry about—definitely nothing to be ashamed about as well. I understand, and I don't judge nor hate you for that."

"You do?" Patrice looked up, hope taking a seat on her face.

"What can I do to help?"

"Well I have a crazy idea. You did say you've wondered what it would feel like."

"No, the answer's no. I'm not letting no man fuck me."

"Well then, teach him to fuck me, see if he gets it. These niggas be portraying dick like that's what makes a man. Why not school one of them? You don't have to fuck him, but you could, if you feel like, but no pressure, yeah?"

"Hell, I've got a freak on my hands," Nia said as she burst into mad laughter.

"You did bring this side of me out. Baby—" She started coming close. "One and done. Let's do this together, please."

"When I said I'd do anything for you, I meant it. Nothing is too big, but we'll never speak of this again. Promise."

"It'll be like it never happened."

"Good. Have anyone in mind?"

"Remember that guy I used to date in college? The football player, Will?"

"Yeah."

"He's coming to town this weekend. He once mentioned he thought you were hot. I bet he still feels that way. He's a super nice guy, quiet even, and plus, you'd never run into him again. Come on, he's perfect—let's fuck him."

And that was it. A simple "no" would have been the right thing to say, but it was a night of cravings and fulfillments; hardly anything right was expected. So

Nia said yes, and Patrice went ahead and phoned Will to relay everything.

An excited Will screamed from his end of the phone. He had wanted to cancel his trip back home because it costed too much, and nothing exciting really happened at Fairhope, Alabama, but now if he could get on a plane at that moment, he certainly would have.

I will just sit and watch, Nia thought to herself.

The doorbell rang at 7 p.m., exactly as expected. Nia was the one to open the door. Will was there, as hot as ever. The man always looked good whenever she saw him. The high-neck black jacket outlined his thick muscle and abs.

He was assessing her as she was assessing him. She was in a T-shirt and jeans as well, having on slip-ons instead of heels. She refused to dress, secretly hoping that Will would have some other appointment and not show up. From how he looked at her, he found her beautiful.

"Am I late for the party?" he asked with a smile on his face.

"No, man, you are just on time. Please come in!" replied Nia.

Will entered the house and took off his jacket and boots. Nia guided him to a sofa and stood, seeing his face clearly. His masculinity stopped at his chest; from his neck up, he looked beautiful with his oval-shaped face and short shiny black hair combed to the back.

"Patrice is still taking her time to dress upstairs," Nia started.

At the same time, Patrice appeared at the door in deep blue lingerie and heels. Her long brown hair fell on her back and accentuated her makeup and red lipstick. Nia gasped. Patrice grinned and glanced at Will, who was staring at her, mouth agape.

"Hey, Will! How is it going?" said Patrice.

Patrice took a seat beside Will as Nia left the room and returned with a beer for him. Immediately, she announced that she would set the rules: Will wouldn't touch Patrice or her unless he was permitted. He would watch them first, then join in later; no spanking, no gagging, and for sure sex toys were allowed.

She smiled when she saw them nod in agreement with a glint in their eyes. She stood up and led the way to the bedroom.

"Get undressed!" she ordered.

Will wasted no time in getting naked. She had never seen a naked man up close before, having a real cock dangling in front of her. She looked away and told him to have a seat in the chair positioned at the end of the bed. Will had a confused look on his face but did as she requested.

Nia went to the dresser and pulled out two sets of handcuffs and two silk scarfs. She handcuffed his right hand to the chair, then his left. She spent a few moments securing his legs to the chair.

He was now completely bound, unable to move.

"Um, can I ask what you have in mind?" he asked curiously.

She took his hard dick in her hand and stroked it— the length and thickness fascinated her. She leaned like she wanted to kiss him deeply but bit his ear lobe lightly and said, "No!"

She went to where Patrice was standing and watching impatiently. She straddled her and gave her a deep, lustful kiss. Patrice kissed her back.

"Ready?" she whispered into her ear.

"Hell yes!"

She gave Patrice another deep, hungry kiss as her hands found her breasts and she began to play with them. She wasted no time in removing her lingerie quickly as Patrice helped her out of hers, leaving on only her black pants and bra. In no time at all, they were both on the bed making out in front of Will, while he looked on with a huge smile on his face. He tugged on the cuffs, only to be reminded that his role in this activity was to watch.

Patrice got on to the bed slowly, making sure that Will had full view of her pussy as she crawled to the center. Nia positioned her head between her legs and started to lick her pussy. Her tongue found her clit as she flicked it and teased it before sliding two fingers into her hot wet pussy.

Nia had long fingers and could reach deep inside her body. Her tongue licked her clit hard and fast. Patrice started to moan loudly. She loved it when Nia ate her and had no problem showing her appreciation vocally. Nia's tongue continued to lap at her clit as her fingers pushed hard into her pussy. She could taste her juices readily flowing from her body.

Will watched them closely. His cock was throbbing and aching for attention, and there was nothing he could do about it. He would have broken the rules if he wasn't cuffed to the chair.

Patrice moaned louder as her breathing became heavy. Nia grabbed her tits and pinched her nipples, sending her over the edge. Her juices shot out hard from her body onto Nia's lips and lower jaw. Nia moved beside her in the bed and kissed her deep. She could taste her cum mixed with beer on her lips as their tongues locked in a lust-filled kiss. Nia got up and walked over to Will.

"Are you liking the show, baby boy?" she asked in a taunting voice.

"Please tell me what I have to do to be unbound so I can join in?" he pleaded.

Nia said nothing. She leaned in and kissed him, making him taste some of Patrice's cum on her lips and tongue. He greedily sucked on her lips, savoring Patrice's sweet nectar.

"In time you will be allowed to join but not yet!"

Before she went back to the bed, she went to the dresser and brought out a pink dildo, long and thick. She had recently gotten it and had been saving it for their anniversary, but it would be perfect now. She walked to where Patrice lay. Patrice's eyes widened at the length and thickness.

Nia told her to get up onto all fours at the edge of the bed. Patrice did as instructed, glancing at Will briefly, with a seductive gaze. Nia turned the dildo on and slowly positioned it at her entrance. While at it, she looked at Will. Deep into Patrice she thrust the dildo and pulled it out. Her pussy was pulsating, throbbing. Nia kissed her lips before pushing it in again.

Will had a full view of Patrice's pussy, how the dildo went in and out, rhythmically, how her cum soaked the dildo and dripped. She was moaning, vibrating each time Nia increased the pace of her thrusts.

"Nia, I am begging! Please let me join in!" he begged as his hand tugged on the cuffs.

"In time, baby boy, in time," she replied with a teasing smile, using one of her hands to play with Patrice's tit.

She told her to get up and lie on the bed. Patrice flopped down, still reeling from her orgasm.

Will could see the fire in her eyes. He had never seen her so turned on before. Nia's hands were still playing with her tits. Patrice continued to look deep into his eyes as she felt the dildo fill her pussy completely.

Her pussy was soaked as the dildo thrust into her faster and harder. Will watched, unable to remove his eyes from the action. The bed was wet with Patrice's cum. He looked back into her fiery lust filled eyes. She used her tongue and traced her lips slowly. Will pulled at the cuffs, hoping to break free, but it was a futile attempt.

She smiled at him, moaning and rolling her eyes in pleasure. By now, Nia had slipped her hand inside her pants and was masturbating herself as well. Thrusting the dildo and fucking herself faster, he could hear Nia moaning now, fitting perfectly with Patrice's yes-yes-yes. He knew that they would soon reach orgasm.

Patrice lowered herself to Nia's pussy, not pulling out the vibrating dildo. She lapped up her juices and sucked her until she reached full orgasm. She sucked Nia through it, at the same time thrusting herself with the dildo and moaning; her eyes didn't leave Will the whole time.

Once Nia felt she'd had enough, she pushed Patrice away, suggesting that he could join in now. Patrice walked over to Will, took his cock into her mouth, and sucked it hard, caressing his balls. She had missed dicks. He tugged on the cuffs hard, trying to grab her hair but was unable to. She could taste his juices forming on the tip of his dick and knew he was going to erupt. She stopped suddenly and gave him a long, hard kiss.

She went back to the drawer and pulled out a blindfold. She whispered something into Nia's ear as she lay on the bed. Nia blindfolded Will while Patrice got the keys from the drawer and removed the cuffs from her ex-boyfriend and helped untie his legs.

"Easy, baby boy," Nia said and guided him to the bed.

She pushed him down and Patrice guided his rock hard cock into her dripping wet pussy. His hands found her tits, and he pinched her nipples hard. She began to ride him slowly first, then quickly, bouncing on him a little too excitedly. Will's hips moved in synchrony with her thrust. Nia tied his hands to each side of the bed and sat on his face, forcing him to eat her pussy.

Patrice screamed as she came instantly. Her pussy squeezed his cock hard as it squirted her juices all over him. Will continued to suck Nia hard and fast as he felt his cock nearing its release. Patrice pulled away and started to stroke it hard. His cock shot a long line of cum all over her face; she lowered herself to suck some of it, laughing satisfactorily.

Another line of cum shot out of his dick and splashed on her tit. She stroked his cock hard and milked all of his cum from it. Suddenly, another blast shot across her chin and neck. Nia orgasmed, squirting on his face, telling him to lick every drop as she held the wall and rode him hard.

Afterwards, Nia and Patrice untied him and removed his blindfold. His face was covered in cum except the part where the blindfold had covered. Patrice offered to bathe first and gave them both a long, lustful kiss before leaving for the bathroom. She heard Nia moaning again, like she'd been holding it back for so long but had lost control.

6

A VERY MODERN CUCKOLDING

BY JADE ST. JAMES

Sometimes, I wonder why Kimajh has to travel on these trips. But then, we need the money, so I rarely complain. He was the only one who ever understood my needs and made them a priority. The other men I'd been with barely had time to get in and get out. They didn't really understand what I wanted when it came to sex. They just wanted my big booty bouncing in their faces as they fucked me doggy style.

I knew I had a big booty. It was the part of me that people often notice first. My first boyfriend, Marcus, was so into it that he couldn't keep his hands to himself for a minute. He would make sure he tapped my ass any opportunity he got. And although I loved him a lot, sex with him was very dull. He only knew how to kiss, press my booty, and turn me over for doggy. I never got to explore all the other things I saw on the Internet and what my friends told me about their boyfriends. So when he went away to college, I called it quits with him.

Darren was a bit better, but he couldn't stop gushing about my booty.

"Are you sure your mother didn't take you for surgery when you were little?" he asked while we were fucking one day.

"No!" I replied hastily. "This booty is natural!"

We both laughed about it then, but he kept asking, and I couldn't stand it anymore. The breakup was nasty and left me vulnerable. I desperately wanted a man who would love me for who I was and not for my booty. So I fell into the hands of the same set of guys I never wanted to get involved with. They preyed on my vulnerability and left me in a big mess. My sex life suffered so much that I began to doubt if I could ever be anything other than the girl with a big ass.

It was a hell of a life until I met Kimajh. At first, he wasn't so appealing. He looked like one of those regular guys who had no interest in sex. There was nothing so special about him except the fact that he was very funny. I had just gotten out of another bad breakup then and decided to hit the bar when we met.

"Hey" was all he said that night.

I simply nodded and went back to drinking with my friends. His group seemed loud, and he was the center of attention, but I could have cared less. Later in the night, I started to get a headache and told my friends I had to leave early. I walked to my car and found Kimajh smoking outside. I instinctively reached out, and he smiled before handing the smoke to me.

"I should warn you—" he was saying.

"I know it's pot," I answered without turning in his direction.

The joint hit after a few drags. My headache disappeared, and I became very horny. Kimajh must have noticed because he tried to excuse himself, but I dragged him toward me and kissed him passionately.

First, I was very high. And then, there was an emptiness inside of me that I desperately needed to fill.

"Are you sure you want to do this?" he asked hoarsely.

I shut him up with a deep kiss and opened the car door. Without wasting time, I pinned him to the back seat, kissing him like my life depend on it. He was surprised when I reached for the condom in my car and was about to slip it on him.

"What are you doing?" he asked.

"Let's be done with it," I replied with a sigh.

"It doesn't work like that, lady," he said with a shocked look on his face. "Here. Let me."

He made me lean back and began to kiss me slowly. The hunger in his kiss was deeper than mine, engulfing me like molten lava. He seemed to know every part of my body, trailing hot kisses as he passed through the familiar routes. I didn't know how or when, but he had discarded my clothes already. I didn't want to open my eyes for fear that he would stop. I just let him take control of me.

"Are you okay?" he asked when he noticed my eyes were shut tightly.

I just nodded and kissed his lips. His hands began their movement now. From my neck to my shoulder, he rubbed me gently. Then he trailed a long line to the twin mounds on my chest. He pinched my nipple a bit, and I felt something jolt inside of me. It was surreal, like a lightbulb breaking into a million pieces. I felt myself reach for an invisible hand, drawing myself close to an edge I never knew existed. And just when I thought it was all over, his lips touched my nipple softly, and he whispered incoherently against it.

I felt a soft, moist liquid burst from under me as I struggled to keep myself from tipping. I didn't know it, but I was moaning loudly, attracting attention from a few others who stood around the parking lot. But either he didn't care or he was just caught in the moment. Kimajh kept sending waves of pleasure all over my body.

"Please," I whispered after I caught my breath. "Please."

He didn't answer. He just pinned my hands behind my head and continued to trail kisses all over my body. Then his mouth went below my navel, and I felt the tingling again. This time around, I succumbed to the feeling and let out a tiny squeak as my fountains burst again. I was lost and unable to find myself. But I loved this. I didn't want to be found at all.

Kimajh must have read my thoughts because his mouth closed over my center, sending me into another whirlpool of pleasure. He sucked and kissed. He slurped lightly and slapped my ass as he did so. I was totally gone, and I didn't care. All I wanted was for that moment to last forever. I came twice, and he kept going until I had melted like butter. But he still didn't stop. Then he raised his head to look at me. I saw a mix of evil and danger lurking behind those eyes of his. But they didn't scare me. They enticed me instead.

"Want some more?" he asked seductively.

I couldn't even answer. I just leaned back and submitted myself to his will.

That day marked the beginning of a new era for me. I craved everything Kimajh had to offer. I was his for the taking, and I wasn't scared. Even though I had doubts about what could become of us, I would have gone to the end of the world to be with him. It felt like an arrangement for me, but to my surprise, Kimajh made it a reality. He told me he wanted nothing more than to be with me always.

He told me to move in with him, and our sex life blossomed into something entirely unique. We tried lots of sex toys. We had fun doing a lot of things I never thought were possible. I was no longer the girl with a big ass. He made me feel like so much more than that. We were out on a date one fateful evening when he asked me a very serious question.

"Will you marry me?" he asked.

I didn't hesitate. I said yes, and he kissed me passionately. That day, we had sex in the restaurant bathroom, and also in the taxi on our way back home. I had never had so much sex in a day, but that day, I made sure I had all the fun I wanted.

A few weeks later, Kimajh traveled to Houston for a job. I missed his dick more than anything else in the world. We would often FaceTime, but that was never enough. I needed him to bury his huge dick inside my throbbing cunt. I wanted him so badly that each time his face showed up on my screen, I would start dripping.

"Babe, I miss you," I told him on the call one day.

"I miss you even more," he replied. "I wish I was there with you right now."

"It gets so cranky without you to caress it," I told him while bringing the camera down to my pussy.

He smiled and told me to hold on. He reappeared later with a cock ring I had gifted him a few weeks back.

"You took it with you?" I asked in surprise.

"It's a piece of you that I'll never let go of," he answered with a chuckle. "I miss you so much."

He placed the phone where I could see his naked-ness and stood with his huge dick staring back at me. I felt my boobs begin to protest the lack of touch that had plagued them since he left. My hands strayed to my pussy lips, and I began to rub slowly.

"Gosh," I said softly. "I miss you so much."

He was jerking off, moaning my name as he reached for a peak I knew too well. I dipped a finger into my pussy and licked it. It smelled good and tasted very nice. I would have done anything to have Kimajh right in that moment, but I knew he was too far away. I closed my eyes and imagined his hands on my boobs, caressing them softly. I began to mumble, calling out to him as he also tried to reach for me. We both knew each other's bodies well. I knew that by calling his name, he would get lost in the same maze that was currently tormenting me. I also knew it would drive me crazy, and that felt so delicious. I also craved his cum in my mouth. It gave me joy whenever he came in my mouth.

"Baby," he groaned. "I'm about to come."

He was sweating profusely, and I could see the beads of water trickling down his chest. I missed my baby so much, and watching him felt so satisfying.

"Come for me, baby," I urged. "Come all over my tits."

He exploded with great force. There was cum all over his broad torso, slowly running down his navel.

"Sorry about that," he said breathlessly as he cleaned the cum off.

"I wish that was in my mouth," I said with a purr.

He laughed. I could tell he missed me too. His face was contoured with desires that he couldn't hide from me.

"Turn around for me," he commanded.

I turned, slapping my ass cheeks against each other.

"That booty calling my name," he joked. "I miss slapping those cheeks."

"All yours, pappy," I replied.

How words were turning me on, and I couldn't hold on any longer. I grabbed my favorite dildo and set it before the camera.

"Do you want me to ride it?" I asked him like a baby.

"Not yet. I want to guide you all the way in."

He was my master, and I had never doubted him once. I gently sat, waiting for his instructions.

"I want you to oil up," he began. "And make sure it's all over."

I quickly grabbed the scented oils we often used. I loved getting oiled.

"Don't be too quick," he cautioned. "Do it very slowly."

I could see his dick getting hard again, so I made the

action slower than usual. He was playing with his balls now, pulling them up and down slowly.

"All over those tits, baby," he said softly.

I applied a portion of oil on my tits and rubbed them. The feeling sent shivers down my spine. This was supposed to be Kimajh's hands on my tits.

"Nice and slow," he kept saying.

I opened my eyes to see he had slipped the cock ring on.

"Yes," he whispered as I rubbed the oil over my belly and all the way down to my pussy.

"Oh, Kimajh," I moaned.

My fingers slid into my center and I felt him there, guiding me all the way in. I increased the speed of my thrusts just as he would if he was fucking me.

"Oh my goodness!" I screamed as I reached orgasm.

It made me vibrate and sent chills all over my body.

"Damn! That was hot!" I told Kimajh.

"I wish you were here, honey," he said back. "I miss you a lot."

I sighed. I was tired of having to do this alone. I really needed him.

"It would be nice to have you around," I told him. "I feel so empty without you."

"I know, baby," he said. "Why don't we go over the wedding budget again?"

I knew he was doing this just to make me feel better. He knew I would get upset if we continued to talk about how we missed each other.

"Okay, so we need to finalize the guest list," I said, flipping through my notebook.

Kimajh nodded, his eyes focused on the screen.

"Right. How many people do we want to invite?"

"I was thinking around a hundred," I replied, biting my lip nervously. "But with the way things are, we might have to cut that down."

Kimajh's expression turned thoughtful.

"Yeah, that's true. Maybe we should consider having a smaller wedding and doing a big reception later when things calm down."

I nodded in agreement, feeling a sense of relief wash over me. I had been worried about how we would survive after the wedding since Kimajh had only just gotten a better job.

"That's a good idea. We could still have our closest family and friends there and then celebrate with everyone else later."

Kimajh smiled, looking pleased with the plan.

"Exactly. And we can save money on the catering and decorations too."

I chuckled.

"Always thinking about the budget, huh?"

He grinned. "Hey, weddings are expensive. We have to be smart about it. Besides, we wouldn't want to be broke after getting married."

I leaned back against the cushions of my sofa and sighed as I watched Kimajh's face on my phone screen. We had been talking about our wedding plans for what felt like hours, but it still didn't feel like enough.

"I miss you, Kimajh," I said softly, feeling a lump form in my throat.

"I miss you too, Deja," he replied, a wistful look on his face. "I wish I could be there with you."

I nodded, feeling the weight of the distance between us. It wasn't easy planning a wedding, and it was even harder doing it without him by my side.

Kimajh suddenly grinned mischievously, interrupting my thoughts.

"Hey, you know what? My friend Kelvin looks just like me. Maybe you can invite him over to keep you company."

I rolled my eyes playfully, feeling a smile tug at the corners of my lips.

"As if anyone could replace you, Kimajh."

He laughed, and the sound filled my heart with warmth.

"I know, I know. I'm irreplaceable."

We continued to talk for a while longer, discussing the details of our wedding and dreaming about our future together. Even though we were miles apart, it felt like he was right there with me, holding my hand and guiding me through the planning process.

After the call ended, I went into the bathroom to take a shower. The water was cold, but I didn't bother to turn on the heater. I wanted to feel the calming effect of the water on my body. It was the only way I could douse the fire Kimajh had lit under me. Because it had been minutes since we'd both come, and I still felt very horny.

The next day, I decided I wanted something unique with Kimajh. He didn't quite get me, so I told him I was going to drive to meet him, and he laughed.

"Don't be silly," he told me. "You don't even know where I am."

I laughed out loud, but there was pain in my voice. Why did he have to be away for so long? He knew I had needs. Why punish me this much?

"Hey," he said to me after a few minutes, "I'll be home soon."

"You better be," I threatened playfully.

"You know I want nothing more than to be with

you," he said. "And I want to make sure you're always satisfied."

I smiled at him.

"You know what? I want to watch you get satisfied," he added suddenly.

"What do you mean, Kimajh?" I asked, still laughing.

There was a knock at the door, and I told him to give me a few minutes. I noticed the smile on his face but didn't think much about it. I opened the door, and his friend Kelvin was there.

"Hi, Deja," he said as I made way for him to come in.

"Hey. Kev. What's up?" I asked him.

H suddenly pulled his shirt off, and staring back at me were the tightest abs I had ever seen. He was hot. Too hot for me to keep my eyes off him.

"I'm not supposed to say anything," he said as he walked toward me. "Set the camera so he can watch."

I was too dazed to even ask him anything. I just positioned the camera as instructed. Kimajh gave me a wink right before Kelvin lifted me to the sofa. He undressed me slowly, taking his time to feast on my body. I was supposed to protest. I wanted to protest. But my body simply failed to respond to my thoughts.

Kelvin took off his shorts, and I realized he wasn't wearing any briefs. His dick was huge, almost the same size as Kimajh's. Was this what Kimajh meant when he said they looked alike? Despite my previous inhibition, I desperately wanted this huge dick inside me.

He laid me back and placed a finger to his lips for me to keep quiet. He worked from my waist up to my chest, kneading every muscle in my body until I felt like jelly. Then he went to the kitchen and came back with some ice, which he placed in strategic places all over me. The icy feel of the ice made me hornier than before. I was totally lost in a maze of desires.

Kelvin took off the first piece of ice with his tongue, slurping loudly as he did so. The feel of his tongue on my naked body made me shiver a bit. He was just as good as my Kimajh!

He licked off what remained of the ice and proceeded to do the same to the others. I squirmed, feeling helplessly turned on. He placed a cube of ice on my pussy and lightly rubbed it against my clit. I moaned, wanting desperately to touch him. He brought the ice back to my clit and left it there for a bit. Then he sucked it off again. I couldn't bear the teasing and tried to grab him. He put my hands back beside me and went back to work. His tongue was cool as it settled on my clit. He took a nibble and then sucked on it. The room began to spin, and I moaned loudly.

"Oh, God!" I cried loudly. "Fuck!"

He was eating me out with so much vigor. It was so good, and I wanted more. He stopped a bit, tapped my ass, and continued. I squirted, but he didn't stop. He simply waited for me to regain consciousness before he increased the tempo. I came again and again, and each time, it felt like I was just starting over.

He finally stopped and motioned for me to sit. He brought his huge dick to my mouth and gestured for me to suck it. The bulging piece of meat felt so filling as I took it in. I sucked and slurped noisily, hearing Kimajh urge me on from the phone. Then Kelvin held my head and began to fuck me in the mouth. I rubbed my clit as he did so, enjoying the feel of his dick slamming against my throat. He came in my mouth, and I swallowed it all.

We moved closer to the camera, and I bent over for him to enter me slowly.

"Show him what you can do," Kimajh said.

Kelvin rammed himself into me with each thrust, matching my pace. He held both of my hands back and went deeper and faster. I squirted three times, but he didn't stop. He was just as dominant as Kimajh. He kept going for another hour before pulling out and turning me toward him. He came on my face and gestured for me to lick everything. I did as instructed. Kelvin got his things and went to take a shower.

I turned to Kimajh, who was furiously jerking off while calling my name loudly. I was super turned on again, and I played with my clit until we both came. I had had some of the best moments with him, but this was beyond anything I ever imagined.

Kelvin came out of the bathroom with his clothes on. He gestured to Kimajh on the phone before blowing me a kiss and walking out.

"Did you enjoy yourself?" Kimajh asked me.

"This is the best time of my life!" I answered gleefully. "I thought you were joking when you told me to go to Kelvin, you know."

"Babe, I told you there's no holding back, right?" he said. "Well, get ready for more adventures when I get back."

I smiled. Kimajh was the best man I could have ever wished for. He knew me and went out of his way to make me happy.

"I love you so much," I told him sweetly.

He smiled so brightly it felt like he lit a thousand bulbs at once.

"I love you too, Deja," he said. "And I can't wait to go on so many adventures with you."

He kissed me good night and ended the call. I got up and went to take a long shower.

7

HELPING OUT THE MARINES
BY LESLIE Z.

Kimberly sat down at her desk, pen in hand, and began to write a letter to Steve. She could feel her heart pounding in her chest as she thought about all the things she wanted to tell him.

"Dear Steve," she began, "I hope this letter finds you well. I have been thinking about you every day since you left, and I miss you more than words can say. It's been hard being apart from you, but I am proud of your work for our country."

Kimberly paused for a moment, thinking about how she could best recount the events of the past few weeks to Steve. She decided to start with the most exciting news. Her sex life.

Steve was particularly interested in her sex life for a reason: Her adventures turned him on. The day they met, Kimberly was out on a date with a guy who was a dick. He made her feel very intimidated and seemed to have an annoying way of talking down on her. Kimberly didn't try to get up or talk back. She just sat there, taking all the insults. So Steve got up from where he was sitting and moved toward the couple.

"I'm sorry, sir," he began calmly. "Could you keep your voice down? The rest of us are just trying to have a nice meal tonight, and you're making that very difficult. Also, there are kids here."

He ended his words with a smile and turned to go back to his table. Kimberly's date was visibly irritated by his interference and couldn't keep it to himself.

"And who do you think you are, pussy?" he asked angrily.

Steve stopped in his tracks and turned around.

"Say that again," he dared the man.

"Who the hell do you think you are, pussy?!" the man repeated.

Steve's fist found the man's jaw with such alarming ferocity that it broke instantly. The man tried to throw a punch, but Steve got out of the way and tripped him. The other patrons were surprised, and some of them brought out their phones to record the fight. Someone had already called the police, and when they arrived, Steve showed them his identity card. He also explained that the man had been causing a scene, and he had to put him in his place. The police arrested him for assault and took him to the station.

Kimberly followed in her car. By the time she got there, the man's lawyer was already trying to get him out. She apologized for what happened, but Steve only smiled and told her not to worry. She stayed until everything was settled, and when Steve was about to leave, she offered to drive him back to his place since he didn't have a car.

"You really don't need to," he protested.

"But I want to," she insisted. "You stood up for me without knowing who I was."

Steve saw that she wouldn't stop, so he went with her to the car. They both fell silent for the first few minutes of the ride until Steve asked if he could stop along the way.

"I need to see a friend," he told her.

"Your babe?" Kimberly asked with a smile.

Steve laughed out loud.

"I don't have a babe," he answered after the laugh had died down. "Used to have one, but she decided I was no longer fun."

"That's odd," Kimberly observed. "What do you mean by that last statement?"

Steve sighed and leaned back in his seat. "We had a little bit of chemistry from the beginning, but she decided it wasn't what she really wanted. Our relationship was rather strange, you know."

"Tell me more," Kimberly said as she made a turn.

"Well, we were both adventurous from the start," Steve began. "She liked the idea of an open relationship, and I wanted the freedom to explore as well."

"Open relationship?" Kimberly asked. Her curiosity had been piqued.

"Yeah," Steve continued. "We both agreed to see anyone we wanted to see as long as there were no secrets about what we did. She would tell me about sex with other guys, how they fucked her, and all sorts of things."

Kimberly could tell he was holding back. She wanted to know more, so she urged him on.

"I need the details," she said with a small laugh.

"If you insist," he said with a chuckle. "She liked gangbangs a lot. I think she once fucked me and three other guys at once. And honestly, I enjoyed myself. I was turned on by watching other guys fuck her from all angles, and that felt very good. As for me, I didn't really like fucking other girls. Just one was enough. But it was more gratifying to watch my girl slutted out by other guys."

Kimberly's head swam with lots of ideas about how she could also have a relationship like this. She was already getting wet thinking about all those dicks slamming into every hole in her body at once. More than two pairs of hands holding her close, caressing her soft breasts. The thoughts almost drove her mad, and she began to see Steve in another light.

"Are you okay?" Steve asked when he noticed her unusual silence.

"What?!" Kimberly asked with a start. "Of course, I'm fine," she calmly said.

They both fell silent then. Steve kept looking at her. He could tell she was disturbed by something he had said, but he didn't know what it was. He decided to push further.

"Was it something I said?" he asked.

"What? No!" she replied hastily.

He had his answer then. It *was* something he had said. She was thinking about what he said.

"You have never been in an open relationship?" he pushed further.

Kimberly sighed loudly. She didn't want to answer, but at the same time, she felt like she owed it to him. Plus, her body was drawn to his masculinity.

She hadn't noticed at first, but it suddenly became clear that Steve often hit the gym. His biceps threatened to rip his shirt off, and his skin was so smooth it looked like butter. His voice wasn't so thick. Just normal. Very normal.

Kimberly also noticed he had a sense of direction. He watched the road keenly and often checked her hand whenever she made a turn. He was definitely the kind of guy she needed in her life.

"I know you want to ask me a question," Steve said suddenly.

Kimberly chuckled. Was it so obvious? She looked in the mirror and realized she was blushing. Her pussy also tingled with excitement, and she had to constantly move her thighs to keep the wetness from spilling.

"Kim?" Steve asked again.

Kimberly finally gave in to her desires.

"Okay," she said calmly. "I am kind of turned on by what you're saying, and I wouldn't mind getting into a relationship like that too. I mean, I love the idea of getting some adventure and all. It really turns me on."

Steve nodded and looked out of the car window. The main reason he had come to Kimberly's rescue at the restaurant was that he really found her attractive. She had big boobs and a moderate ass. Her eyes were seductive, calling to him with a desire he couldn't explain. Her smile was perfect too. He'd gotten a hard-on the moment she touched him earlier at the station, but he had hidden it then. If only there was a way around the awkward situation they found themselves in.

"You said you wanted to stop along the way," Kimberly said suddenly. "Are we there yet?"

Steve shook his head. He was finding it hard to say anything for fear he would say something else.

"Are you sure you don't want us to stop somewhere?" Kimberly asked without looking in his direction. "Somewhere private?"

Steve didn't trust his voice not to betray his excitement. He simply nodded and turned his attention to the road. Kimberly placed her hand on his lap while pretending to be focused on driving. Steve looked at her and chuckled. He knew where this was going, and he liked it. She had initiated the first move, something he had been dreading from the beginning.

"Your place or mine?" he managed to ask.

Kimberly pulled over instead. She grabbed him and planted a deep kiss on his lips. They both moaned softly as their lips explored and brought their passion to the surface.

"Wait," Steve said, stopping momentarily. "Do you think it's safe around here? Someone could be coming."

Kimberly looked around. She had parked beside an old building with nothing but a door at the entrance. There were old cars around the parking area, probably abandoned long ago. The door of the building also showed signs of rust. There was nothing else to suggest they could be seen.

"I don't think so," she finally answered before resuming the kiss.

Steve was a good kisser. He teased her, welcomed her hunger, and fed her everything she wanted. The car was cramped, but they seemed to care about getting their hands on each other instead. Kimberly pulled her hair back and went for his zipper. She would have loved to explore more, but she desperately needed him inside her first. When the zipper came open and the briefs came down, she was met with a dick that looked bigger than her arm.

"Damn!" she exclaimed. "You're packing."

Steve simply shrugged. He let her take his dick in her mouth and threw his head back to enjoy the feeling. Kimberly was tender, almost like she was worshiping his manhood. She sucked on it first, then she gave him a blow job while returning to the kiss.

"You're good with your hands and your mouth," Steve murmured.

"Wait till you see what this pussy can do," she replied seductively.

Steve managed to recline the car seat so they would have enough room. Kimberly had gone back to sucking his dick, but she didn't stay there for long, and he knew why. Her pussy juice was dripping, and when he dipped a finger there, it was as wet as anything he could think of.

"Come and fuck me," Kimberly said. "I don't think I can wait any longer."

She swapped positions with him so he could spread her legs wide. Her pussy arched itself toward him, begging to be pounded. Steve went in slowly, making sure he filled the entire length of her center.

"Oh God!" Kimberly moaned. "You're stretching me out!"

Steve loved the way she moaned. It showed she was ready for him. He started with slow and rhythmic movements, gazing into her eyes as he went in and out. Then he increased the tempo a bit. He watched her eyes roll and felt her quiver as he picked up speed.

"Yes, Daddy," Kimberly moaned louder. "Fuck this pussy. It's yours, Daddy."

Steve knew he had hit the jackpot when he heard her talk dirty with him. She had the spirit of adventure inside of her, and he was going to make sure it was well fed.

"Who's your daddy?" he asked, just to make sure he still had control.

"You, Daddy," Kimberly answered. "Choke me, please."

Steve held her thigh with one hand and her neck with the other. Kimberly shot her tongue out, obviously enjoying the moment. They both continued to talk dirty, rising with the notes of their bodies. He found a place where they could both sustain the momentum and kept her there. Kimberly came first. Her orgasm was bone-shattering. It sent her into a frenzy, and she began to sob quietly.

Steve followed a few seconds later. His grunts came fast, and his breaths came heavily. He didn't bother to pull out, either. He just poured all his strength inside her.

"You know, I was going crazy while driving," Kimberly confessed later.

They slept in each other's arms despite the discomfort from the car seats. Steve nodded as she talked. He could have done with a cigarette right then.

"You're a beast," Kimberly continued. "I don't think you should be going home just yet."

Steve laughed. "I don't think so either," he replied. "So where do you want to go?"

She drove him to her apartment, where they had three more rounds of amazing sex. Kimberly was a loud moaner, and it filled Steve with so much joy. He liked to be in control, and she was happy to oblige. After the sex, they showered together. Kimberly gave him a blow job in the bath, gulping down his cum as soon as they were done. Then Steve got dressed and left.

They continued to fuck each other until they decided to make things official. Steve asked if Kimberly wanted to be exclusive or they could keep it open since he wanted her to have the luxury of enjoying what others could offer. Kimberly agreed, happy to share him with any girl that came along. A few months later, Steve went off on an assignment.

The first few weeks were terrible for Kimberly. She desperately wanted him around, but she knew there was no way she could have that. During one of their numerous phone calls, Steve asked her to write him letters instead.

"Why?" she asked. "I can always send you texts."

"No," he protested. "I want to read everything and anything. I want to know more about that guy. What's his name?"

"Richard," Kimberly answered.

"Yes. Richard. You told me his dick was huge."

"Unusual for a white guy, but yes."

"I need you to tell me all about it in all your letters," Steve ordered. "I want to read your letters and feel like I was right there with you."

And that was exactly what Kimberly did. She fed him with all the details of her sex with Richard.

Richard was a basketball player she had met in a bar a few weeks before Steve left. He seemed like a nice guy, so when he started hitting on her, Kimberly went with the flow. They ended up at his apartment, and he fucked her till she was sore. When she told Steve about it, he was very happy. So she kept telling him about Richard even after he left on his trip.

"All right," Kimberly said later. "I'll write to you every week."

Steve hung up, and she called Richard to ask if she could come over to his crib.

"No problem," he answered.

Kimberly decided to go without putting on any underwear. She almost drove over the speed limit in anticipation of what she was going to get. When she got to the door, Richard was already waiting.

"I ordered some hot wings," he told her. "You might want to eat something later."

Kimberly laughed. She walked in and unzipped her

dress. Richard's mouth flew open as soon as he saw she had nothing under it.

"You amaze me every day," he said before grabbing her close.

Their kiss was passionate and left Kimberly panting. Richard got out of his shorts and sat on the couch. He told her to get on her knees and suck him.

"Yes, Daddy," she replied.

Ever since she met Steve, Kimberly had made sure to improve her head game. She not only sucked now. She also loved to be throat-fucked. It made her squirt as she got hammered deep in her throat.

"Come on, bitch," Richard commanded. "Suck this fucking dick."

She was right in the middle of it when the doorbell rang.

"Shit!" Richard exclaimed.

"What's wrong?" Kimberly asked, cleaning her mouth.

"My friends were supposed to come over today," he explained. "I totally forgot about them."

"Well, they're here now," she told him. "Wanna get the door?"

Richard scratched his beard.

"I don't know," he answered slowly. "I mean, you're supposed to write to Steve today, right? I don't want Abe and Blake spoiling your story."

"Abe and Blake from your basketball team?" Kimberly asked excitedly.

Unknown to Richard, she had always fantasized about what those guys would be like in bed. She had seen Abe's dick once while he was playing and his shorts came all the way up. He was not huge, but she liked what she saw. It was a chance to finally get her wish, and she wasn't prepared to lose it.

"Let them in," she told Richard.

"Are you sure?" he asked. "I mean, I'm down for anything but...you know."

"Don't be silly," Kimberly replied with a laugh.

Richard got up and went to the door. He opened it and shook hands with his friends.

"Well, boys," Kimberly said as they all walked in. "Let's see those dicks."

She stood before them naked, ready to tango. Abe's eyes flew wide open, but Blake didn't seem to mind. He dropped his pants first. Kimberly clapped with glee.

"Abe?" Richard called.

Abe turned to look at his friends. They were both naked. He shrugged and pulled off his clothes as well.

"Who's going first?" Kimberly asked with a chuckle.

Blake stepped forward and grabbed one of her breasts with his strong, firm palm. He gave it a little squeeze and slapped her ass.

"Let's see what you got," he said with a smirk.

Kimberly bent and took his dick in her hand. She gave it a few rubs until it was hard enough for her to insert in her mouth. Blake nodded as she swallowed him whole. He turned to the others who stepped forward to surround Kimberly. Abe rapped his dick against her face, and she held it with one of her hands.

Richard came from behind and just stood watching. Kimberly knew she had to satisfy all three of them. She sucked on Blake and rubbed Abe's dick until they both began to moan. Then she raised her ass up and turned to look at Richard.

"Why don't you fill up that hole?" she told him.

Richard nodded and grabbed a lube. He squirted a little in her asshole and inserted his dick.

"Yeah," Kimberly said softly. "Oh. That feels so good."

Blake held her mouth to his dick to keep her from talking too much. She let him fuck her mouth freely while she played with Abe's dick. Richard increased his tempo, and she found it hard to keep steady. So they all moved to a large couch in the middle of the living room. Abe stood by her side so she could work her hands on his dick while Blake and Richard took opposite sides. Kimberly came twice as Richard fucked her ass. She begged him not to take his dick out as she was enjoying his thrusts. Blake took that as an invitation to fuck her throat too. He stuffed his dick all the way in and began to thrust violently.

"I'm coming!" Abe announced.

Kimberly increased the tempo of the hand job, and he spilled all over her body. She loved the feel of his hot cum; it drove her passionately insane.

"Come stuff your dick in my pussy," she told him.

The others allowed Abe to insert his dick into her pussy while they stayed opposite as she gave them both hand jobs at the same time. The men threw their heads back, enjoying the magic her hands worked on them.

Abe slapped her clit hard, and it made Kimberly squirt. He rubbed his dick against her clit until she was done squirting before he went in again. This time around, he rode her like an animal. His thrusts were faster than any she had ever had before. It was almost like he was a machine. He kept going, oblivious to what was happening around him. He was so lost that he didn't know he was grunting loudly. But rather than get frustrated, Kimberly was enjoying the whole show. She loved his energy and tried to match it as well.

Blake tapped Abe to wait a bit while he got under Kimberly. He stuffed his dick in her asshole, and Abe put his in her pussy. Not to be left out, Richard stuffed her mouth with his dick.

"Hmmm," Kimberly moaned. "Yes!"

They all fucked her crazily at once, and she loved every moment of it. It was a crazy scene, one she had always imagined. She didn't know it would come to her so quickly.

Richard came right in her throat, and rather than let him pull out, she grabbed his dick and let him pour it all in. Then she let him off and swallowed hard.

"Fuck me like a bitch!" she shouted at the two others.

Blake increased his speed, almost throwing Abe off, but the other man found his rhythm as well. Blake's grunts were as loud as the orgasm that traveled all over Kimberly. She quivered as he spilled into her. Abe didn't stop for anything; he kept going until he also spilled inside her.

"Damn!" Kimberly said to them all. "Now I'm filled with cum."

They all laughed, and Richard tapped her ass.

"You're awesome," he commented.

"We're just getting started, boys," Kimberly told them. "Now I want you all to fuck me one after the other."

Richard started first. He turned her over and began to fuck her doggy style. Kimberly had multiple orgasms from his thrusts alone. She melted in his hands like butter but got up after each orgasm to continue. He met her speed and passion with his animalistic grunts. When he came, she quickly turned so he could spill on her face. Then Blake took over. He also spilled on her face. Abe took over from him and fucked her in so many styles that Kimberly lost count. He was very creative and versatile. He hit her where it mattered and sent her into a fit of bone-shattering orgasms. After he came on her face, Kimberly rubbed it all together and licked them. Then she swallowed.

"She's crazy," Blake told the others, and they all burst out laughing.

"You have no idea," Richard added.

Kimberly was elated. This was the kind of moment she'd always wanted to have. It made her feel very fulfilled. Her whole body wanted more, and she knew she was supposed to listen.

They continued all night until they were all tired. They had a shower together and ended up fucking again. Finally, they all crashed on Richard's bed, bodies strewn over each other. Kimberly was smiling to herself while the boys slept. Her whole body ached, but it was totally worth it. She had had the best moment of her life. Steve was going to like her letter that week.

And she couldn't wait for him to get back from his trip.

8

WHAT HAPPENS IN NEW ORLEANS…

BY JENNIFER ABBOTT

I paced from one corner of the room to another, picking things along the way and throwing them into the opened trunk on the queen-sized bed. There was a spring in my step. The cream-painted walls stared at me. The house reverberated with an all too familiar silence, one I had gotten used to since Cal had died on that summer day ten years ago.

On my way back to the closet, I stopped at the large, framed wedding picture hanging on the wall and mused. It had been taken on the day Cal and I got married. Cal was in a blue suede suit and white shirt with a black bow tie. I was in a sleeveless white gown that spread out on the floor around me.

Even without looking at the picture, I could remember his smiling face on that day, especially when he looked at me beside him. The curve in his lips was a glimpse of the joy in his heart. Sometimes, he would whisper in my ear about how lucky he was to have me. With his eyes on me, I felt like the most beautiful woman in the world.

Now he was no longer with me. Fate had taken him away from me on a particular winter day. He had called to say he would be coming home by 8 p.m. instead of 6 p.m. because he had some urgent job to complete. The tiredness in his voice worried me, so a plan formed in my mind quickly. I prepared to relieve him of his stress by giving him a hot bath and great sex afterward.

First, I started by having a nice hot bath. I ran the water, undressed, and slid into the tub. I washed myself everywhere, then pulled out a razor and shaved my legs. Then I pulled out a new razor and shaved my pussy, ensuring that not one hair was missed. Cal liked my pussy to be as smooth as a baby's bottom.

I got out of the tub, dried off, and went to the vanity in the bedroom. I sat there naked and tried to think of a unique plan for Cal, something different from the usual. I sat and looked at my naked body while I thought. I grabbed his favorite cologne and sprayed my neck, a squirt between my breasts, and a squirt on my wrists. Then I moved on to apply my makeup perfectly, like I was going out to an expensive restaurant or somewhere special.

Afterward, I opened my lingerie drawer. Sitting to the side was a box I had almost forgotten about. A few months ago, I had gone shopping for a new lingerie outfit that I was saving for a special occasion, and I could not think of a better time.

I pulled out the box and opened it. I put on the thigh-high fishnet stockings. I attached the clips to the corset and sat before the vanity again, looking down at myself to make sure that my tits were sitting perfectly. The corset pushed my tits up high so there were on display for his viewing pleasure. I made sure the stockings were on straight and the clips were perfectly in line with my sexy thigh.

By the time I was done with dressing, it was 8:10, ten minutes before he would be home. I checked myself in the mirror before going to wait for Cal at the door. More ideas ran through my mind as I waited. We would make out on the couch before moving to the room for proper sex.

As soon as the clock struck 8, I went to stand behind the door, waiting for him to push it open. I missed him. Every time he left the house to work, I couldn't wait for him to return. My anxiety increased with each hour that passed by. In the early hours of the morning, my fears were confirmed. Cal was dead. A truck had crushed him. He wasn't just gone for a few hours, but forever.

No matter how much I mourned, I couldn't move on with my life. I abandoned my pursuit of a degree in English. Also, I quit my job as a freelancer and rejected every proposal from interested men. Cal's deep green eyes and cute smile, the first reason I had fallen in love with him, wouldn't leave my mind.

No other broad shoulders and thick muscles appealed to me like his. The memories of him and our time together kept repeating on me. Most especially the day before his death, when he brought home a bouquet of fresh daisies. We both adored flowers.

So I decided to visit all the places we had planned to visit together. We had made a list of them. I looked away from the picture and at the small book in my hand. It contained the names of the places Cal and I had dreamed of going to see together, mostly scrawled in Cal's handwriting.

Each time, I took some of his clothes and his favorite cologne. I'd visited all the places listed except the last one. My eyes landed on the last two words at the bottom of the book: *New Orleans.* I smiled. Luckily, this wasn't just the last place on the list, but a place that coincided with our tenth anniversary.

Perhaps after this, I would be able to move on—get a job, get a master's degree in English degree, and fall in love again. I glanced up at the picture, into Cal's deep green eyes and smiling face. He seemed to be smiling at me like he was urging me on.

I dropped the last items into my trunk: two pairs of pajamas each for Cal and me, his favorite cologne, and a complete set of lingerie wear—the same one I'd worn the day he died. On second thought, I grabbed the robe from the hanger and then zipped up my suitcase.

As I walked down the road, I looked around. Birds were chirping, and some traders were haggling in French at a store. From a flower shop close by, I perceived the scent of fresh flowers. They looked just as fresh as when I rested my eyes on them. Their scent seemed to stand out and at the same time, meld together.

"Oh, sweet. Can you see the flowers? Do you perceive that?" I said, gazing into the sky, hoping to see a sign —a star, a rainbow—anything to confirm that Cal was with me now.

The sky stared back. The clouds floated by, ignoring me. Disappointed, I sighed and kept walking. A guy was playing piano and singing in a bar nearby. The music made me soberer. I couldn't hear the lyrics of his song, but the sound of the piano filled the air.

The sound of the music faded the farther I went. Unshed tears brimmed in my eyes, but they wouldn't spill out. Suddenly, I halted and looked back at the line of stores on my right. My eyes fixed on one of them with the name in big block letters: *Psychic Medium*. The name seemed to get bigger somehow, pointing to something unclear. I spun around and approached the storefront impulsively.

It was dark inside the store except for the colored lights that flicked on and off from the bulbs hanging high in the ceiling. A woman was sitting behind a table. From my distance, her face was unclear, as well as the top of the table. A faint smell of incense hung in the air. I took a few steps closer.

There were two empty chairs in front of the table. On it were different sizes of bottles and spices of several colors in powdered and solid form. A candle sat in the middle of the table, burning dimly. The woman's face seemed to glow in the candlelight. Her eyes were wide open, staring into space and not blinking. How scary!

"Cal is here with you," she said in a slow brassy voice as I turned around to leave.

I paused in my steps and peered at her. "Excuse me, ma'am?"

"Call me Madame Rose," she corrected.

Her voice seemed to echo in my ears, or perhaps I was just imagining it.

"Take a seat."

Pushing aside the several questions that ran through my head, I walked to a chair and sat. Her eyes remained unchanged, though they now seemed to be staring at me but not really staring at me.

"What do you know about my husband, Cal?"

"He is sitting right next to you."

I glanced to my right. The seat was empty.

"Madame Rose—" I started to express my disapproval.

"Shh, he is saying something to you. Can you hear him?" she interrupted, letting her wide eyes leer at me for a moment.

"No, I can't," I replied, even more amused.

"Look at him. He is in a blue shirt rolled up to his elbows. Oh, his eyes are a deep green."

I glanced at the empty seat again, more confused. "What is he saying?"

"I don't know. I can't hear him, but he is staring at you. His message seems important. Listen to him, Jada." She reduced her voice to an irritating whisper.

"You know my name?" My chest thumped louder in my ears. I replaced my sobriety with anxiety, confusion, and anger. What the hell was happening?

"He is holding a bouquet of daisies." She was staring at the empty seat with that faraway look, like she was really seeing him. "He is holding it out to you. Take it."

For the third time, I gazed at the empty seat and saw nothing. Worked up to full panic, I got up, ready to get away from this woman.

"Collect it already, Jada."

"I don't know what this is about, Madame Rose, but I am not going to be part of it. Cal was my husband, but he can't be here with me. He is dead." I paused and swallowed. A pain clutched my throat. I had just admitted the truth I had been running away from all these years.

"He is still holding out the daisies. You are—"

"Damn you, woman! You know nothing about Cal and me, so stay clear!" With that, I stormed out and headed back to my hotel.

She was right, although I hated to admit it. The last memory I had of Cal was him holding out a bouquet of daisies to me. How could she know that? How did she know our names?

The scenes replayed in my head: Madame Rose's voice, the things she said, the candle, and the fragrance of incense, alongside everything that happened at Psychic Medium. I wanted to get it all out, together with the anxiety and anger that I felt. Sleep wouldn't do it. So I got up, gathered my toiletries and robe, and went into the bathroom.

After filling the bathtub with warm water, I got into it and sat. With vigor and anger, I scrubbed on my skin like I could wash off every memory of today out of my mind so that only the image of Cal's handsome face would fill my mind. As I scrubbed, I cried, feeling rage fill my chest.

I felt angry at myself, at no one, at everyone, and at the world. Why did it have to be my Cal? The tears kept flowing, with small sounds of pain escaping from my mouth; not the pain from scrubbing on my skin but a familiar pain that clutched at my chest.

Eventually, I rinsed the soap off my body and got out of the bathtub, wrapping a robe around my body.

For a moment after I stepped out of the bathroom, everything else seemed to blur around me. I wiped my eyes with the edge of the robe, half stumbling around the room. A mild, earthy scent permeated the air, like the scent of daisies.

"Daisies?" I thought out loud. Or was I imagining that because of what Madame Rose said?

But it was real, live on my dresser. When I pulled the robe away from my eyes and looked around, I saw it sitting there: a bouquet of daisies, just like the one Cal had given me. It hadn't been there when I left for the bathroom. *Who dropped it here?* I thought, moving toward it. My chest thumped again.

I touched the tip of the flowers, half hoping they would disappear; however, they didn't. With shaky hands, I picked up the vase from the table, holding it a few inches from my face and at the same time assessing it. The next moment, I headed for the door to throw it out, but I caught sight of a figure on my bed. I paused and blinked. The person sitting on my bed was staring at me with deep green eyes, accompanied by a warm smile. Cal? Was this really Cal?

"You made it to New Orleans. That was my plan for our 10th anniversary."

It was Cal! No one else would have such a deep bass voice. I leapt to the bed to meet his lips in a kiss. I missed him—the taste of him, the feel of his lips on mine, everything about him—and I wanted to explore every part of him.

I pecked at his lips a few times. They were warm and soft. I withdrew a bit and traced the place I had just kissed with my finger. He wrapped his arm around my waist. I put an arm around his neck. His face seemed to glow, or was it the light overhead?

Our lips met again in a hot, wet slide, this time more intense than the first. I prodded his lips open with my tongue, tasting the sweetness of his saliva. It was as sweet as milk. I brought my other hand to his face, pushing my tongue deeper into his mouth.

There was something otherworldly about his body, apart from the fact that his skin glowed. The heat was rising between us. I removed my hands from around his face and brought them to his well-built chest. I didn't want to care about anything else. He sucked on my lips eagerly, making slurping sounds.

While we were still kissing, I maneuvered his trousers down to feel his erect cock over his shorts. He responded by reaching his hands over to the same spot between my legs. We slowly massaged and rubbed. My thighs spread wider to allow his middle digit to slip inside my pulsating pussy. My vulva throbbed a heavy beat as my whole engorged sex dripped with desire.

With synchronous movements, he fingered me while my slim fingers circled his erection, feeling its urgent heat. I sucked on his lower lip as I stroked his cock. His free hand kneaded my breasts and pinched at my nipples. I moaned into his mouth. He pulled away and leaned to have a look at my pussy. The emotion in his eyes was unreadable, a combination of amusement and something else.

"I am sorry. It's not as smooth as you like it," I choked out, embarrassed. "I didn't think it was necessary. If I knew you were coming, I would have had a good shave."

"Shh, it's fine. You are still so sweet," he whispered, kissing my nipples.

"Your eyes have not—" the 'changed' got lost in my

mouth as the sensation of his palm rubbing against my clit tipped me over the edge.

I insistently reached into his shorts and slid my hand up and down the length of him. I moaned thickly, feeling my pussy clenching and contracting around his thrusting finger, the rich, wet fluid of my cunt oozing into his hand. He thrust my hole faster with his fingers, making me moan thickly. My curiosity was at the peak. I couldn't wait any longer. I pulled out his dick. It was fat and long, just the way I remembered it. It made me desire to feel him inside me.

"Fuck me, fuck me already."

"Say please."

"Please, baby, fuck me," I cried.

His dick entered my hole and filled me. At a measured pace, he thrust in and out. I moaned while I moved my hips in synchrony with his. He picked up the pace, pumping me faster. My loud moans became screams as I reached climax. Cal ejaculated at the same time. I felt his cum trickle down my pussy and around my thigh.

But we were far from done. Cal pulled out of me. I looked down at him, disappointed. His wet tongue emerged from between his lips and wiggled at me playfully before he lowered his head to my damp, throbbing pussy. He lapped our juices dripping from my pussy, eagerly and quickly.

In a short time, I was moaning again. My pussy was on fire; new juices were being created. Cal continued to lick me hard as he slid two fingers deep into my hole. I moaned loudly as my fists clenched the bed sheets. I was about to climax again. He kissed around my labia, sucking and nibbling lightly. Then his tongue returned to my clit, where he licked me feverishly, his fingers pounding my pussy hard and fast.

"Argh! Yes!" I screamed loud.

I came again hard. My juices shot out of my body onto Cal's face. He leaned forward and slurped them up greedily. I screamed, caressing his hair. Later on, he fell to the bed, panting. I claimed his lips again, tasting our mixed cum on his lips and tongue. My hands found his cock, falling slightly. Slowly, I stroked him back to an erection.

I stroked it a few more times before taking him into my mouth. First, I put half of his nine-inch monster dick into my mouth, took a moment to relax, then slowly let it reach the back of my throat. I paused for a moment, then repeated it again, taking him even deeper into my throat. All the time, I gazed into his eyes.

I slid my mouth up his cock, licking the underside of his shaft with my tongue as I slowly took his entire cock into my mouth and past my throat. This time, I allowed him to linger there for a moment. Cal looked deep into my eyes with a sexy, pleading expression. He wanted more. My head bobbed up and down on his massive cock while my hand stroked the base of the shaft.

Still maintaining eye contact, I licked the tip of his cock and took it back into my mouth. I moved my hand away and let the head reach deep into my throat. Cal's breathing was getting heavier each time I repeated it. After some more deep-throating, I felt his hot cum splash at the back of my throat. It was my turn to swallow his load greedily. Also, I let some splash on my face. I still wanted more. I sat up.

"Just one more thing," I announced.

He looked at me mischievously, smiling ever so brightly. I leaned to kiss him. At the same time, I plunged myself onto his cock. My pussy was boiling as I fucked him hard and deep. I screamed out instantly as my cum spilled onto his erect cock. But I didn't stop. I continued to ride him hard as my juices dripped.

Cal reached up and grabbed my tits hard as I came. He pushed his hips up hard so his cock could reach deep into my body. I pushed him down hard and rode him faster. I continued to scream out loud. Cal was groaning too, watching as my tits bounced freely. Soon he erupted inside me. I could feel his cock pulsating in my body as he filled me deep.

I sat on his cock, waiting for his load to be released before I pulled out and collapsed beside him. We laid side by side, saying nothing. I was still reeling from my orgasm. It was like old times. Present and past seemed to meet to become one. Cal's arm found my shoulder and pulled me to him. I could hear his breathing against my face.

"I love you so much, Jada." Cal was the first to speak.

I lifted my gaze to meet his before giving my response: "I love you too."

"I wish you were with me." There was a tinge of sadness in his voice.

"But I am here with you," I interjected.

Cal sighed, staring at the ceiling. His face glowed like a light was hanging down over his head.

"I am going to move on, baby, and I want you to do the same," he finally let out, exasperated.

"You are not going anywhere, are you?"

"We are in two different worlds. You should find love again, get married, have kids. Remember, you always wanted to pursue a degree in English. You should do that now."

"Please stay with me. I want you by my side, Cal." I held on to him, determined never to let go.

"Yes, I will always be with you, but I want you to move on. I want you to be happy again." He kissed my lips, stopping me from protesting further.

I jerked awake with a start. The light was on; my robe was secured around my chest. Was it a dream? Had I really seen Cal? I wondered, getting out of bed and looking around for a sign. A bouquet of daisies on the dresser. Yes, the daisies, I recalled. There was nothing on the dresser.

Even the fragrance of daisies was gone. Had I imagined all of that? It must be somewhere, anywhere, I thought, looking around. Finally, I stopped at the mirror and peered at my reflection in the glass. A daisy hung loosely behind my ear.

CONCLUSION

If you enjoyed this collection of erotic stories, please take a moment and leave us a review. Every review helps us find new readers. Share the sexy fun!

Until next time, my queens, be well!

Sincerely yours,

Jade

www.ingramcontent.com/pod-product-compliance
Lightning Source LLC
Chambersburg PA
CBHW050517160726
48003CB00001B/349